WHILE YOU WERE OUT

SHORT STORIES OF RESURRECTION

Proudly Presented By

WWW.COLUMBUSCOOP.ORG

Edited By

Amy S. Dalrymple & Brad Pauquette

Pauquette ltd
dba Columbus Creative Cooperative
1658 Harvard Ave.
Columbus, OH 43203
www.ColumbusCoop.org

DEVELOPMENTAL EDITOR
Brad Pauquette

COPY EDITOR
Amy S. Dalrymple

PRODUCTION EDITOR
Brad Pauquette

PROOFREADER
Mallory Baker

All fifteen stories included in this work are previously
unpublished.

Cover photograph by Raymond Riedel, 2012.
Printed with permission.

ISBN 978-0-9835205-5-9

Printed in the United States of America
1 3 5 7 9 10 8 6 4 2

CONTENTS

*To the writers and readers of Columbus, Ohio, may
you live again in symbiotic harmony.*

INTRODUCTION

My dad used to own a worthless Ford F-150 truck that he named Lazarus. Much like its biblical eponym, it would seemingly perish, only to revive again a few days later.

Once a year or so, a turn of the key produced the dreaded clicking, or no effect at all, and then the beast would sit for days or weeks, bathing in the regenerative juices of the sun, cleansing itself in the rain, rusting in what little un-rusted real estate remained above the fenders and on the bumpers, and refusing to start day after day.

But, as if the god of old two-tone pick-up trucks knew that it was its last chance, on the morning that "call a tow truck" was scribbled in my father's planner, presumably with no destination but the scrap yard, one last-ditch turn of the key would rev Lazarus to life as if he were brand new.

Columbus Creative Cooperative collected stories about resurrection for this anthology. The only rule for the stories that were submitted was that something must die and then come back to life. The resurrected thing could be a person, an animal, a machine, or even something abstract, like a project, an idea or a relationship.

I expected that we'd sift through dozens of stories about zombies, vampires, and other typical sorts of the undead, but after all of the stories were collected, we were met with an amazing variety of stories that transcended all genres. As it turns out, we didn't select a single story that deals with any of the typical "undead" that saturate our culture. You won't find a single vampire or zombie on these pages.

Instead, you'll find fantastic stories of people, hopes, dreams, relationships, animals, and even a car, that die and come back to life. You'll find one story, "Rerun," that introduces a whole new type of undead character that I think you'll enjoy.

These stories are adventure, drama, fantasy, science fiction and even a couple of wonderful pieces of creative non-fiction.

Every story was carefully crafted by a writer who lives and works in Central Ohio. We collected submissions from all over North America and the English speaking world, but at the end of the day, we received an exceptional amount of qualified content from our neighbors here in Ohio, and we used it exclusively.

These stories were written by people you run into every day. They were written by your bus driver, your waitress, the local daycare coordinator, a few students and even a couple of retirees.

We've done our best to assemble a great variety of stories. Not every story will fit your preferences, and that's OK, but every story is an excellent example of work in its particular genre, and I think you'll appreciate every single one.

Writers of all levels are encouraged to participate with Columbus Creative Cooperative, whether through our publishing or our workshops. We don't publish every story that comes through our door, but we do our best to provide an environment in which every writer can grow and develop his craft to a professional level.

Any writer who's tried to sell a novel or submitted a story to an anthology knows well the process of death and rebirth. Every rejection letter and failed project is a tragedy, but a few days or weeks later, we approach the blank page once again and birth a new character or revive an old one into the word processor.

Resurrection may seem outlandish, I thought it was and I wasn't sure if we'd collect a single story, but it seems that we're surrounded by death and rebirth. Not only Jesus Christ and Jack Bauer on *24* either, rebirth is a part of nature and a part of our relationships, our bodies are constantly regenerating on a cellular level, and there are some things in our lives, like broken down Ford F-150 pickup trucks, that just won't die.

Please enjoy the stories of *While You Were Out: Short Stories of Resurrection*.

-Brad Pauquette

Director, Columbus Creative Cooperative

For more information about Columbus Creative Cooperative, please visit **ColumbusCoop.org**.

Brenda Layman

Brenda Layman is an award-winning freelance writer and a prolific member of several Central Ohio writers' groups, including the Outdoor Writers of Ohio. She wrote her first story, "The Turtle," at the age of three. She dictated it to her mother and then bound the hand-written text into a construction paper cover illustrated with crayon and secured with a copious application of tape.

A native of Ashland, Kentucky, Brenda has lived most of her life in the Columbus, Ohio area. She is a graduate of The Ohio State University and is currently working on a Master of Communication and Marketing degree at Franklin University.

Brenda and her husband, Mark, have a small internet business called Select Authors which develops and promotes indie authors and provides website design and management services to small businesses.

"Sprout" is Brenda's second published fiction work, following "A Fish Story," which appeared in the CCC anthology, *Across Town*. Both stories are Fantastic Realism, a genre in which the real and the imagined merge into an unfamiliar world where anything can happen.

Brenda writes for *Pickerington Magazine*, *Ohio Valley Outdoors*, and *Columbus Underground*.

Read her blog at select-authors.com.

SPROUT

By Brenda Layman

Janet Jones double-checked to make sure she had unplugged both the toaster and the coffee maker before leaving the house. She stepped outside onto her front porch, locked the door behind her, and then tried the knob firmly to make sure it was secure. On the few steps along the front walk that led to her carport, she took stock of the front of the house with its clean windows that looked out onto a small garden where plants grew in orderly rows. Then something caught her eye. It was a tiny plant, just a sprout, really, that was out of place, sticking up from an almost unnoticeable crack in the walk. Janet bent down, pulled it out, and tossed it under one of the neatly trimmed evergreen bushes that hid the concrete block foundation skirting her small brick house. Then she opened her bag, took out a tissue, and wiped away imaginary stains from her fingers.

Shortly before six o'clock that evening, Janet returned home from her job at the insurance company. She parked her car in the center of the carport, turned off the ignition, got out and locked the door. Then she tried the door twice to make sure it was secure before she started along the front walk to the porch. Janet didn't park in the one-car garage anymore. Some of Brian's stuff was in there. She narrowed her eyes. The sprout was back, and it looked at least as vigorous as it had that morning. "You! Back again?" she said. She bent and pulled up the new sprout, taking care to get roots and all. She looked at the little plant, hoping to identify it, but she was at a loss. Its two heart-shaped leaves were a reddish color, like poison ivy in autumn.

Janet took the sprout indoors with her, walked into the living room and found *Common Plants of North America* on her bookshelf. Her books were arranged in order of size, not alphabetically. An alphabetical arrangement would have resulted in a terribly unsatisfying situation, with books of differing dimensions aligned in helter-skelter fashion. She looked at several pages with illustrations that resembled the plant in one way or another, but not one was a perfect match.

"It must be a non-native. Probably invasive," Janet muttered. She would probably need to use weed-killer to get rid of it completely, she thought, as she put *Common Plants of North America* back into its proper slot. After dinner she searched the internet until bedtime, but she could not identify the little sprout.

The next day was Saturday, and that was cleaning day. Although Janet never allowed her house to get really messy, on Saturdays she mopped and vacuumed, dusted and polished her little home until it shone. It was laundry day, too. When she had four blouses ironed nice and crisp, she carried them to her closet and hung them exactly two inches apart. On the left side were her things, purses on the top shelf, blouses, slacks and skirts hanging from the rod, and shoes arranged neatly below. On the right side were Brian's things, equally neat and orderly. She pulled a cloth from her pocket and knelt down to dust Brian's shoes.

Janet sighed. Brian had left quite a number of things behind. Even though he had not returned for them, she still took care of them. It was a little bit like having him still with her.

Brian was fun. He was spontaneous and outgoing. People loved him, and when Janet was with him, people loved her too. She was surprised when he noticed her at the office and started hanging around her desk. She was more surprised when he asked her out to lunch, and completely amazed when their relationship blossomed into full romance.

After several months of dating, he moved in. Things went

well for a while, but then Brian began to seem different to Janet. He didn't laugh as often. She sometimes caught him giving her an odd, puzzled look. She tried to relax, tried to be comfortable with his habits, but he didn't seem to care about keeping things the way they should be. He dropped socks on the floor. He hung his towel crookedly in the bathroom. He put dishes into the dishwasher with bits of food still clinging to them.

One day when they came home from work, Brian pulled off his tie and dress shirt as soon as he walked in the door. He walked to the kitchen, draped the shirt and tie over the back of a chair, and then opened the refrigerator and took out a beer. He turned around to find Janet standing there with the shirt and tie in her hands.

"What are you doing with my stuff?" Brian asked.

"This is my home, not a filthy frat house," she retorted.

Brian said nothing, but he took the shirt and tie upstairs to the bedroom and put them away. The next morning Brian announced that he was planning to leave. Janet would never forget the scene. They were standing in the kitchen. Brian was holding his favorite coffee mug, the red one with the kangaroo on it. He was barefoot, sporting boxer shorts, a T-shirt, and an agonizingly sexy morning shadow.

"Janet, we need to talk," he said.

"I don't want to talk," she replied. "I don't want you to say it."

"Janet, you know it's time. What we had was great, but sometimes even great things don't last forever."

"It will," she said. "It will last forever." But Brian only looked at her, so sad, so kind, as he slowly shook his head.

"Sometimes things just stop growing, Janet. Don't make this harder than it has to be. Let it go."

She shook off the memories. After she finished cleaning inside, Janet went outside to see if the garden needed trimming or weeding. She stopped short as she stepped onto the front walk. The invasive plant, whatever it was, had returned. Three reddish sprouts stuck up out of the mulch beside the walk. Janet fetched her spray bottle of weed killer from the basement and returned to the garden. She pulled each of the three little plants up, roots and all, squirting a liberal dose of weed killer into the holes where they had been. "That will fix you," she said.

Clouds gathered before dawn on Sunday morning, and soon sheets of rain lashed across the windows of Janet's little house. She stood in the kitchen in her bathrobe and slippers, drank coffee from the red kangaroo mug, and watched water run in streams down the street and along the gutters.

How strange, she thought, that all this water will wash along and carry the dirt from my garden into the river and out to sea. The thought unsettled her. She thought maybe she should plant tomatoes in the spring. Then the soil and rain and sun of her garden would become part of the ripe, red tomatoes, and when she ate them it would all become part of her and be with her forever. She liked the idea. It rained all day, but Janet found plenty to do. She had work from the office, and when that was all done she had books to read, and there was always television.

On Monday morning she started off for work as usual, but when she opened the front door she saw a most disturbing scene. The rain had nourished the invasive plant. It had spread throughout the garden, and dozens of the little sprouts thrust up from the ground. "There must be an underground root system, rhizomes or something," Janet said to herself. She glanced at her watch. There was no time to deal with the plants; she had to be at work on time. Janet was always punctual.

A pile of papers was waiting for her when she arrived, and it wasn't until lunch that she could search the internet again for solutions to her weed problem. Erica, a co-worker, stopped by Janet's desk.

"Got weed problems?"

"Yes, some kind of exotic invasive."

"Have you sprayed it with weed killer?"

"Yes, but it doesn't seem to be strong enough."

"Is that what you used?" Erica gestured toward the image on Janet's screen. "That stuff is strong enough to kill anything." She leaned over Janet's shoulder and put a Styrofoam cup half-full of coffee down on the desk. A brown ring appeared around the base of the cup. Janet gritted her teeth.

"It worked before," Janet replied. "But not on this plant."

"Maybe you'll have to dig out the roots. Bet you wish Brian was still around, so you could get him to do it." Erica saw the cold look on Janet's face and stammered, "I'm sorry. Bad attempt at humor."

"That's all right," Janet said. "You're right, Brian would have done it. But I guess I'll have to do it myself."

"Weird how he just took off like that, without telling anyone."

"He told me," Janet replied.

"Yeah," Erica conceded. "I guess he just told the person he was closest to, and figured you'd tell the rest of us. Some people just don't like good-byes." She took her cup and walked away, leaving Janet to wipe up the wet, brown puddle with a tissue.

Later that day, Janet felt a strange weight in the pit of her stomach as she turned onto her street and drove toward her house. She pulled the car into the driveway and stared. The plants were everywhere, some of them two or three feet high. She parked in the center of the carport, got out of the car, locked the door, checked it twice, and then turned to face the plants.

"I will fix you," she said.

"Who you talkin' to?" It was Mrs. DelVecchio, Janet's neighbor. "And what in the world are those weeds growing all over your yard? I've never seen anything grow like that. You get rid of those things before they spread over to my yard. I already had my two lawn treatments for the year, and they won't come back and spray again for free."

More neighbors had gathered on the walk in front of Janet's house. Mr. and Mrs. Cartwright with their young son in his stroller, and Mr. Evanovich with his schnauzer, Bingo, had stopped to stare at the unusual weeds. Janet felt her heart pound faster. She turned away.

"Don't worry, Mrs. DelVecchio," called Janet. "I'll get rid of them." Mrs. DelVecchio retreated to her own front porch, and the neighbors continued on their evening walks. Janet went inside, changed into jeans and a T-shirt, and fetched her shovel from the basement. She worked and sweated until dark, digging up each of the plants, roots and all. She carried them into the back yard, piled them up, and burned them in a fragrant, smoky fire with red-and-yellow flames. Mrs. DelVecchio called over from her back porch, "That ought to do it!"

Janet retreated inside, wiped her shovel until it shone, and then hung it in its place among the carefully ordered tools in the basement. Then she tiptoed to her immaculate bathroom to wash off the garden dirt that was smeared across her forehead, over her hands and arms, and embedded under her fingernails and in the fine lines of her fingertips. She thought about the tomatoes she planned to grow and she put a fingertip into her mouth, tasting the soil.

She looked in the mirror at the reflection of her sweaty self, and the sight reminded her of Brian on hot summer days, his hair curling into damp circles, a light trickle of perspiration running down into the hollow at the base of his throat. She remembered the salty taste of his sweat, and the way he would hold her close and whisper to her, and she wished they could have gone on like that forever. She closed her eyes, remembering, feeling the dirt on her hands and face, smelling it, the smell of earth and musk and things that lived in the rich decaying matter, and suddenly she couldn't bear to let it go. She took the soil on her body to bed, lay down and wrapped herself in scent and taste and memories until at last she slept.

She woke early, but lay in her bed for another hour, watching dawn light up the sky and dreading what daylight might reveal. At last she dragged herself into the kitchen, poured hot coffee into the red kangaroo mug, and walked to the front door. She stood there for a moment, wanting to look but not wanting to see, before she turned the knob and pulled, both knowing and fearing the thing that was growing in her garden.

It was back, as she knew it would be, bigger and more aggressive than ever. The plants were everywhere, up to eight feet high, with reddish pearls of dew dripping from luxuriant leaves that nodded gracefully in the breeze.

"Hey, what on God's green earth . . . !" She heard Mrs. DelVecchio exclaiming. Janet shut the door and locked it. As she stood behind her locked door, she felt her heart pounding wildly. She jumped at the sound of the phone, then ran to her nightstand, picked up the phone and stared at it until it stopped ringing and went to voicemail. The number was Mrs. DelVecchio's. Then Janet dialed the number of the insurance company.

"Hi, this is Janet. I'm taking a sick day today. I have a migraine."

Janet went back to bed. Her lights were off and the shades were drawn. She pulled the covers over her head for good measure. The plant was outside, she reasoned. It couldn't reach her there, in the bed that she and Brian had shared. She had always felt safe when he was beside her. She closed her eyes and thought about him, and about how he was the only thing that had ever made her abandon self-control. She remembered the look on his face after he drank from the red kangaroo mug for the last time.

CRACK! Janet's eyes opened at the sound, and she watched, horrified, as a crack moved up from the baseboard of her bedroom wall toward the ceiling. CRACK! The lower, right-hand corner of the window shattered, sending spider-web lines diagonally across the pane. The plant was coming for her, attacking the house, squeezing the foundation in its powerful roots, crushing wood and concrete in its encompassing grasp. The timbers of the house frame groaned as the relentless roots forced them apart. The crevice in the wall widened. Janet couldn't take her eyes off the crack that opened wider and wider, and the slender, white root-tip that slid through it, into her bedroom, and began to snake its way toward her. Two more white roots followed the first, twining themselves up the bed frame from the floor to the head board.

Janet threw back the blanket and slid out of bed. She ran down the stairs to the basement to fetch her ax. She stumbled back up the stairs to the front door, wrenched it open, and leaped into the jungle that had once been her neat front garden.

The plant was enormous. It had become dense and woody, with thick trunks that towered overhead and a canopy of broad leaves that shut out the sunlight. Janet flung herself at the nearest trunk, swinging her ax into its flesh. Blood-red sap gushed forth, and the tree shuddered.

"You can't, you can't!" Janet screamed, hacking left and right at the plant. She was only vaguely aware of the small crowd of neighbors who had gathered on the sidewalk. The plants' giant roots began to heave out of the ground, and the plants, thus

deprived of their holds in the soil, began to fall. Janet hacked
and chopped at them, digging her toes into the upturned soil. An
enormous plant began to list to the side, and Janet watched its giant
root burst out of the dirt, leaving a yawning, black cavity open to
view, a shallow grave filled with neatly wrapped packages. She felt
hands on her shoulders, pulling her back from the hole, and she
struggled to free herself. Blind with panic, she swung out with the
ax toward whoever was restraining her and she felt the blade bite
into flesh again.

Janet looked up and saw the neighbors who stood in a semi-
circle around her, a jury of her peers, white-faced and frozen with
horror. She realized that they would judge her for her actions,
for acts she could neither control nor prevent, and they would
never understand. She dropped the ax and sank to her knees, then
stretched herself out on the ground, thrusting her hands into the
soil, burying her face into the dirt, letting it into her mouth and
eyes, breathing it in.

Ben Orlando

Benjamin David Orlando lives in Bexley, Ohio with his wife and a variety of animals. Due to the veritable eco-system residing inside his apartment, his home is not ordinarily available to visitors.

Ben is certain that one day he will be awarded the National Book Award for a book about a book about National Book Awards. Thirty years from this day he will also dominate the future sport of cage writing, drop-kicking his foes, nailing his metaphors and choke-holding his passive verbs until they tap out and cry "Active!" He will become the heavy-write champion of the world, but his battered brain will stink like boiled kidneys until the day when only one memory proves itself far superior to all of the others: this story, in this anthology, published by this creative cooperative. This prophecy is 85% accurate.

He would like to thank his fellow Columbus Creative Cooperative members for putting together such fine books, and for not insisting on meeting him at his home.

Ben works at Columbus College of Art and Design, and loves Columbus with all of his heart.

THE MISSING HOURS

By Ben Orlando

*Imagine a man raising the dead, healing hundreds from
crippling injuries, feeding thousands from a few scraps,
calming a raging storm and walking on water, and
nobody writing about his deeds for forty years. This is
the case of Jesus of Nazareth.*

-Thomas Mulhaney

I was a writer, and I pissed off a lot of people with my words.
I knew that much when I stepped out of the woods two days ago. I
didn't know I was on the edge of a sparsely-housed Italian suburb
two hours northeast of Rome.

It was a warm night, considering I wasn't wearing pants, only
a torn suit top and polka-dot boxers. GQ worthy, no doubt. I don't
know why I'm joking. It's not funny. But it's absurd, and if we
can't laugh at the absurd, we might as well die.

I stood for a while at the edge of the woods, staring across
the two-hundred feet of patchy lawn that led to a patio and a small
two-story home. Through the open patio door I could see a man in
a recliner watching TV, slurping from a wine glass. His laugh was
dense, how a gorilla might laugh.

At some point I turned back to the woods and tried to
remember where I'd come from. I probably would have done
something differently if my mind hadn't been so dense, like a
soaked sponge. But I wasn't thinking at all, so like a moth attracted
to the light, I turned back towards the house again and walked
mindlessly towards the glow of the TV.

A minute later, I stepped into the living room. The Italian man
was slouched in a green lounger watching something with a laugh
track. He would have to turn left to completely see me, but after
a few seconds he caught me out of the corner of his eye, turned,

15

and stared for ten or twelve seconds more before mumbling "*Che cazzo,*" and jumping out of his chair. He tripped over the hassock and fell twice on his way to the kitchen.

His reaction was warranted. I was a stranger who'd walked out of the woods, across his patio and into his living room, dressed in a soiled gray suit jacket, with a white dress shirt underneath and a green tie hanging loose around my neck. No pants and no shoes and no socks.

I could feel greasy hair down to my shoulders, and a beard thick and hot on my face. I knew who I was. Edward Jacob Louis. Born in Pittsburgh. 1975. Almost drowned in the Dead Sea. Author of two duds before hitting a nerve with my first bestseller, *Jesus, Biography of an Average Man.* I just didn't know where I'd been for the past five months, or where I'd just come from.

"Please," I said. My voice sounded far away, in the next room in the closet, maybe. The Italian man was in his forties, tall like me but his hair was brown and slicked back, and he was heavier, maybe two hundred and thirty pounds, at least forty of that in his stomach. He wore a white t-shirt over a pair of olive dress pants and black, expensive-looking shoes shined to a buff. The stubble was dense around his mouth and chin. He was more or less well-groomed but quickly falling apart as he trembled behind the island that separated the kitchen from the living room. He grabbed for a butcher knife from the block and missed, and grabbed again, and blinked repeatedly. Next to him on the counter was a nearly empty bottle of Tuscan Rosso.

"I'm not dangerous," I said, but he didn't seem to hear me. He looked down and mumbled something, licked his lips as his hands continued to tremble and then he raised his eyes before raising his head. It's hard to explain the feeling of knowing you're the cause of someone's terror. You're the Boogeyman. The smallest part of me felt empowered, that I could have this kind of impact on someone. But the rest of me felt ashamed because in his shoes, I wouldn't

16

talk to the stranger. I would run.

"Do you speak English?" I asked. The man just stared at me, chin down towards his chest and mouth open. "English!" I screamed. It just came out. I didn't speak Italian, but the fact that he didn't seem to speak English infuriated me.

I took a step forward and he screamed, *"No mouvi!"* and knocked the bottle of wine onto the floor with his elbow. He jumped when it shattered and then looked at me as if I'd just kicked his dog.

As my head began to unfog, I thought of a possible way out of the mess I'd created, and scanned the room. To the right, I found what I was looking for. A bookshelf, and it was on the side of the room opposite the kitchen and the man with a knife. He watched, motionless, while I crossed the beige carpet, my bare feet leaving dirty tracks.

The bookshelf was ten feet wide and six feet tall, crammed with paperbacks, colorful hardbound mysteries and thrillers, and magazines. This guy, I thought, didn't seem like a reader. He seemed like a high-end insurance salesman, the kind of guy who might punch an old lady if she deserved it. To cement this view, when I turned back to see what he was doing, the man had a new bottle of wine on the counter, miraculously opened. He just stared at it. Just stared and mumbled.

I turned back to the shelf and searched the spines, careful to sneak a peek over my shoulder every few seconds. I thought he would call the police, but he just stood there, left palm flat on the counter, right hand with knife bobbing up and down, looking at the bottle of wine, looking at me.

I almost cried—I pushed down the convulsions in my stomach and throat—when I saw it on the shelf: the orange spine, the title, translated for the Italian market, *Gesu Cristo: Biografia di un Imbecile.* I never understood how they'd gotten "moron" from "average man," but I was never so happy to see a copy of my book in any language. It wasn't actually so strange to find a copy here so soon after the publication. No one more enjoyed dishing the dirt on Jesus than the Italians, and my book dug in deep.

Based on recent discoveries made by several prominent German and Greek archeologists, and deductions by a few dozen leading scholars, including Marcos Levine, the book refutes the existence of Jesus as any kind of paranormal being. According to these new sources uncovered in two sealed-off storage rooms belonging to the "fiddling emperor" Nero, Jesus was sometimes conniving, and even hostile, but he was no more and no less than a man.

Many Italians would love nothing more than to absolve themselves of the sin-by association committed by their great ancestor Pontius Pilate. If Jesus was simply a mortal man, they could wash off at least some of the blood. Of course, said Gore Vidal in 1995, "More people have been killed *in the name of Jesus Christ* than any other name in the history of the world." That's a tough pill to swallow knowing Jesus was just like you and me. Still, I thought they'd be more on my side than against me, and the sales in Italy proved it.

When the hate mail started to fill my trashcans, I changed my outlook once again—any publicity is good publicity. So goddamn positive. So self-delusional. Attitudes like that can kill you.

I pulled *Jesus: Biography of an Average Man* from the shelf and looked at the back inside jacket flap, at the confident, clean-shaven man with the short black hair and shit-eating grin. Standing in the jittery Italian's home, I couldn't see myself, but I knew I looked nothing like the man on the book jacket. As I stared at the photo, memories began to return: pushing through a crowd near the Vatican the last days of my book tour, angry people shouting, throwing things—eggs, beets, tomatoes, and cloves of garlic— cameras flashing, quite a few unified boos and a tall, white-haired man in the background, wearing a miniature red hat and matching red robe. He was either a cardinal or a man dressed as one, and he was staring at me.

Philo of Alexandria lived from 20 B.C.-50 A.D. and was a prolific Jewish writer of political and social matters, some ancient, many topical, almost all of which have survived. He personally knew some of the historical figures in the "Jesus" texts, and wrote the only existing contemporary account of Pontius Pilate, the famed executioner. Yet Philo never mentions a man named or similar to Jesus of Nazareth.

-Alexander Detremaunt

I turned back towards the kitchen, hoping to convince the Italian man that I was no longer a stranger. I had an identity and the proof in my hands, although there was certain incriminating information in the caption under the photo. I hoped he wouldn't look too hard.

As I turned, I saw the Italian man running towards me, slicing the air with a butcher knife, and I realized I'd been so caught up in finding my book, I'd forgotten to check to make sure he wasn't running towards me slicing the air with a butcher knife.

On the television, two people stopped fighting about something and the laugh track kicked in. I looked down to see a dubbed episode of *Seinfeld* right before the Italian man tackled me. I grabbed the arm with the knife as he fell on me and we dropped sideways onto the carpet. We struggled for a few seconds before his expression changed, from fear and rage to outright confusion.

Suddenly he stopped, his eyes drawn to the book that had fallen to my left. His eyes moved from the photo, to me, to the photo.

"*Si si si,*" I said. "*La libro. Yo, yo, libro de Jesus. Si. Yo.*"

The man was out of his mind with doubt and reconsideration.

I didn't blame him. I felt sorry for him for having to deal with this, with me. We remained in that position for another few seconds until the front door opened and a young woman stepped inside, and, understandably, screamed.

We both turned as she approached, as the man pulled away from me and I scuttled backwards like a crab against the bookshelf. He wobbled to his feet and walked backwards towards the kitchen, never taking his narrowed, bloodshot eyes off me.

"Marcos," she whispered. Her swallow was louder than her voice. She was thin, average height, at least fifteen years younger than Marcos, probably more. And she was wearing some kind of uniform, a beige pants suit. It reminded me of my trip to the Galleria Nazionale d'Arte Moderna in Rome, and the tour guides, mostly women in the skin-tight pants suits, probably a museum strategy to drum up larger crowds. Yes, she was a guide. I imagined her speaking to a tour group in her tight suit and black trendy glasses, her dark hair pulled into a pony tail. She had a mousy little face and was tiny and frail standing next to Marcos.

She looked from Marcos to me, to the broken bottle near her shoes. Since I was close to the TV, I decided to turn it off. I didn't need a laugh track.

"*Usci dal bosco,*" he said.

I had no idea what that meant at the time, but yesterday I bought an Italian-English dictionary across the street, and I still remember all the words. I can't seem to forget anything except what I need to remember.

"He came out of the woods," he said.

"I don't—" she looked at me, at the floor, at Marcos. "I don't understand—"

"He came out of the god damn woods," Marcos repeated, his voice struggling for some control, "and I was about to stab him when *you* came in."

"Marcos—"

20

"Just . . . " He waved his hand in her face, slapped her cheek hard enough, and turned back to me and nearly lost his balance just standing there. "You translate," he said to the woman without turning away from me. I couldn't understand the hatred that was coming from his eyes.

"Who is that man in the book?" he said, while the woman stared at me with no expression until Marcos' hand slapped against the back of her head. "Ask him!"

"What book?"

"Just ask!"

The woman flinched and asked me, "Who is that man in the book?"

"That's my picture, Me," I said. "I'm Edward Louis."

"The author?" she said and looked down, and shook her head. Then she translated. Marcos frowned and sat on the bar stool, put his elbows on the marble counter-top and opened his eyes wide, again and again, as if he were staring into the sun.

"No," he said. "You're not . . . that guy. You look like—"

"Let me shave," I told the woman. "Let me cut my hair and you'll see. Here." I tossed the book across the room. When it hit the floor the woman and Marcos both jumped.

"Hold it together!" he screamed, and she flinched, and then bent with her knees and lifted the book jacket and held the picture up to the light. She looked at me and squinted, and handed the photo to Marcos. "Look," she said

"What?"

"Look."

"What! What!"

"The date," she told him. "I bought that book two months ago. He's dead, Marcos, five months ago." I recognized "five months" and realized for the first time the size of my memory gap.

"No," I said. "Ask me something. I'll quote the book. Chapter one. 'In the history of mankind—'"

"Tell him to shut the fuck up!" Marcos shouted, clanking the butcher knife against the counter while he reached for the open bottle of Chianti.

"Marcos, do you think you should—" the woman began but stopped when Marcos grabbed the bottle and took a swig. He then poured two glasses.

"I'm going to look it up online," she said, her voice a bit louder but not by much. From the floor she lifted a brown leather satchel and pulled out a purple net-book.

"I know Edward Louis," she said to me as she opened the net-book and began clicking. "I saw him in Milan."

"That was me!" I screamed. "I was there … August fifteenth to eighteenth? It overlapped fashion week, right? The theme was … it was Venice. The theme was Venice! You remember?"

She paused, but just for a second. "I'm going to read this," she said to Marcos, who stared at me while he finished the glass and refilled. "I am going to read this," she told me. "Okay?"

I nodded.

"On March fourth, 2011," she said—her English was nearly flawless—"American author Edward Louis, three weeks into his European book tour, was shot and killed by several anonymous men a half mile from the Vatican. Four pedestrians were also killed in the crossfire. The men escaped capture and are still at large. Associated Press."

She slid the laptop in front of Marcos. He mumbled something and her eyes revealed a kind of unfiltered disgust I'd never seen— but that's what it was—before she clicked a few keys and turned to see my reaction. I suppose I was confident in my truth.

"I remember that day," I said.

"How can you?"

"I don't know, but I do."

"Who are you?"

"I remember that day," I told her, "and then nothing, and then

a few hours ago I opened my eyes in the woods, dressed like this.
Please," I said. "Look at my face. Look at my eyes. I am Edward
Louis. I'm not dangerous. I swear I don't want to hurt anyone."

"What did he say?"

The woman translated while Marcos sipped. He seemed to be
pondering something.

"What if we tie him," she whispered. Marcos looked at her as
if she were insane, as if this wasn't the first time she'd caused him
to make this particular face.

"Then we can get a close-up look, make sure."

"Make sure what?"

"What if he's telling the truth?"

Marcos let out a snort and turned from the woman to me and
held onto his reply for the length of a deep breath. "Yeah okay,"
he said, and smiled slightly. "There's some twine in the bedroom."
After taking another generous sip, Marcos put the knife in the
woman's hand and stomped past me into the hall to my right.

"You know my name," I said to the woman. "He's Marcos.
What's yours?"

She looked at the floor.

"Can you tell me? Please?"

"Bea," she whispered.

"Dante's wife," I said.

"No," she said, disappointed. "Marcos' wife."

Marcos was back in less than a minute, binding my hands
behind my back with abrasive twine, then my ankles and knees as
if he'd always fantasized about hogtying someone. Then he leaned
in and studied my face and breathed a cigarette-wine breath up my
nose.

"I can't tell!" he said. "Get me the picture."

She walked around the island and bent down next to him and
handed over the book jacket. For what seemed like five minutes he
looked from the jacket to me to the jacket, to me.

"Let me," she said in a soft, questioning voice. Marcos had to think about it but finally stepped back. She lowered her face within an inch of mine. I smelled a light citrus perfume. Her lips were small, very red but unpainted. At some base level I hated the fact that those lips ever touched his, and suddenly part of the challenge became controlling the movement under my boxers. She was so close, I saw the shiver that began in her neck and worked upwards as her eyes closed and her head tilted slightly.

"You know I'm telling the truth," I said. From her reaction I knew my breath was much worse than Marcos'.

She stepped back and quickly walked around the island and began clicking away at the netbook keys.

"What, what is it!" he demanded and followed her around the counter.

"Let's just ask him a few questions," she said. "Just to be sure. Okay?" And before Marcos could complain, she asked me, "Where were you born?" with her eyes focused on the screen.

I told her.

"What is the name of your ex-wife, the name of your daughter, parents, what funny thing happened when you met J.K. Rowling?"

I told her. I told her. I told her.

She breathed deep and considered the wine in front of her before taking a sip. "You were not killed then," she said.

"I was not killed," I agreed.

"What! What!" Marcos screamed.

She told him.

"What does it mean!" he shouted. "He was killed? He's here? How was he killed? Look. Look up how he was killed. C'mon, do it. What are you waiting for!"

Bea did as she was told while Marcos approached, grabbed me under my arm and yanked me to my feet. While she searched he hauled me onto a bar-stool on the living-room side of the island.

24

"No mouvi!" he shouted loud enough to make both Bea and me jump.

"Well," he said.

"They all say six shots," she told him. "Two in the stomach, one in the chest, two in the arm and one . . . in the forehead. Above the right eye."

Marcos reached over the counter before she finished the sentence, grabbed my chin with one hand and pulled back the hair from my forehead. Bea reacted to whatever he'd revealed like I'd suddenly been declared terminal.

"Okay, look," he told her, and pulled my shirt and jacket over my head.

"Well? How many holes?"

"Three," she whispered. "Just like it said."

Marcos let me go and I nearly fell off the back of the stool.

"Holes," he mumbled, "ask him what he remembers."

She asked me.

"I remember getting shot," I told them and began to explain the finest details of my final memories, the sweet smell of the tomatoes bursting against my chest and a man's scream before the first shot.

"Quiet!" Bea shouted like a librarian might shout. Marcos and I turned and looked at her.

"The articles," she said. "They didn't say this before. Your body," she told me and translated for Marcos.

"Tell me first!" he screamed.

"They dragged it away," she said. "The police just assumed because of how many times you were shot, and where."

"Who?" I asked. "Who dragged me away?"

"I do not know," she said. "It only says several people were noticed dragging you from the scene, and that is the last time anyone saw you."

"We'll see," Marcos said and slid off the stool. In another

three seconds he was across the living room and into the hall.

"Bea," I said. "You don't believe . . . "

"Many people hate you for that book," she said.

For a minute I didn't know what she was talking about. "You read it?" I finally answered.

"I did not believe before that," she said. "You did not change my mind."

"Where the hell is it!" Marcos shouted from what I assumed was their bedroom.

"It's based on new evidence," I told her.

"Not only is Jesus an average man," she said, "but a violent man? A deceitful man? A self-serving trouble maker?"

"Other scientists, other scholars," I said, "reached the same conclusion."

"How does that help people?"

"What?"

"Some people find comfort in Jesus."

"But not you."

When she didn't reply, I continued. "How does it help people to believe life here doesn't have any consequences? How can you live your life here when you think all that matters is worshiping a man? That's the beginning and end of it."

"That is not how I live."

"I didn't say you. It's just the truth."

"Truth," she said. "And where are these other books, these other scholars?"

"On the way," I said, although I wasn't so sure after what happened to me.

"I was going to stop," I told her. She didn't understand.

"Rome," I said. "I was going to do my last stop in Florence. The book tour was going badly, people were just . . . so angry."

"Jesus, where the hell is it!"

Bea jumped slightly but didn't look away from me.

"Do you have the expression," she asked, "sometimes the bull will push you towards the edge where you were already headed?"

"I've never heard it," I told her. She looked down, considering something, flipping through a dozen scenarios in those last few seconds.

She didn't have much time because Marcos appeared a moment later with a self-congratulating smile, carrying the object of his search.

In Ancient times, people did not have many records—few books, no magazines, no videos, no photographs—to keep things straight. Forty years gone by—often a lifetime—may as well be a thousand in terms of accurate recollection. It was in this context that the name of Jesus was pulled from the rubble.

-Emily Hartford Clemence

In Marcos' trembling right hand was a black, polished, modern-looking hand gun. I looked at Bea, who continued to stare down at her glass.

"What do you think I am?" I said.

"Marcos," she said. "What are you doing?" although there was no surprise in her voice.

He extended the gun over the counter, pushed it towards her. She bit her lip. "Why can't you?"

"Because I want you to do it. I cleaned up after you enough."

"You think this is my fault, Marcos?" This time she was surprised. "How is this—"

"Take the gun," he said and grabbed her hand, wrapped her fingers around the handle and stepped back. "Now point it at him."

"Marcos," she said. "There must be an explanation. People have lived through a dozen shots. People—"

"No argument, Bea. No god damn argument. You saw the holes. God, how long are we going to stand here? Point it at him! Point!"

She held the gun with two hands, turning so the barrel was aimed at my nose. She was still trembling but her eyes were calm, almost lifeless.

"I'm going to count to three," he said. "On three, you fire. Ready? Ready!"

She nodded, tears streaming down her face. I thought maybe she'd drop the gun. It looked so heavy in her delicate, trembling hands, the purple nail on her pointer finger jammed against the trigger guard.

"*Uno.*"

"Bea," I said. "You won't be the same afterwards."

"*Due.*"

"Please. Bea, please. Please."

"*Tre.*"

She turned the gun on Marcos, and fired.

He closed his eyes and flinched in preparation and jumped at the sound of the "click." When he realized nothing had happened and opened his eyes, the truth of what had just occurred slowly dawned on him. His bewilderment turned into recognition, which turned into rage. He stepped forward and grabbed the bottle from the counter.

"You dirty whore. I'm going to make you—"

She pulled the trigger again.

I saw the spark at the end of the barrel before I heard what sounded like a very loud firecracker. The shot knocked him back against the wall and the bottle hit the floor. I watched the red stain on the upper half of his white t-shirt grow and grow as he slid down the wall, and I tried to breathe deeply, but only managed a shallow, stuttering inhale. Before I realized what was happening, Bea turned back to me and with sad, pleading eyes, fired point blank into my chest. I fell, or flew, several feet backwards, struck the top of the television set with the back of my head and eventually hit the floor.

When I was twelve, a sixteen-year-old boy named Dvorak punched me in the chest while wearing a set of brass knuckles. The gunshot from Bea was worse, but soon the pain turned to severe heart burn, and then became something like indigestion. And while I lay there it came back, all of the CRACK CRACK CRACK of the shots fired near the Piazza Pia, people screaming, people dragging me away, the cardinal standing in the background.

I don't know how long I was out. Not long. Minutes. When I lifted my head, Bea was at the counter sipping from the same glass. When she saw me move, her eyes jumped, but the rest of her stayed right there on the stool.

"I don't care," she said. "It does not matter to me."

I didn't speak.

She finished the glass and slowly, calmly walked to the sink and pulled on a pair of yellow dishwashing gloves. "I need to live here," she said and grabbed the gun from the counter and stood in front of me. "Here. For however long it is going to be, I want some joy in *this* world. Do you understand? I do not care about anywhere else. I do not care about eternity."

Now I understand what she was talking about, but at the time I was lost.

"He forced me to," she said. "It is his fault. His fault."

"I know."

"I wiped it down," she said. "I placed it in your hands. And in his."

I stared at her, waiting for more. I didn't have a clue what she was talking about.

"The two of you," she said, "had a fight. You shot him, and he shot you, and . . . well . . . you were supposed to die, too."

"Bea."

"I did not think . . . even when he pulled back your hair. But it does not matter. Now it looks like you ran off wounded. With some of his clothes. And you knocked me out and when I came to you were gone. That is when I called the *polizia*."

Taking a deep breath, Bea stared at my glazed expression and clenched her teeth and cracked herself in the forehead with the butt of the pistol. I sat on my side, dumbstruck, while she staggered, grabbed the island for support and shook off the imbalance. A thin trickle of blood slid down her nose and dripped from her chin.

"Bea, I understand," I said. "I understand why you shot him, but you have to help me."

"And there is a jar, two thousand Euros you found in our closet," she said, and lifted the butcher knife from the counter and bent down next to me.

I flinched while she cut through the twine around my ankles and knees. She stepped back.

"Maybe the gun will not kill you," she said, "but it knocks you out, and . . . do not make me do something else. I am sorry. I am very sorry. Go outside."

"Bea, please."

"Go outside," she repeated in the same flat tone.

Hands still tied behind my back, I staggered into the yard. When I was thirty feet away she told me to wait and returned a minute later with a bag full of clothes and the jar of Euros.

"Turn around," she said.

I stared at the dark woods in front of me and felt the blade slice across my thumb as she cut the twine. Just enough to loosen it.

"Stay like that," she said. "Do not fidget for one minute. I am going inside now to call the police. You will not have long."

When I did turn around, she was staring at me through the closed patio door. I didn't know what else to do, so I walked into the woods, eventually found the road, and changed into Marcos' jeans and yellow sweatshirt, and walked. She'd even thrown in

30

socks and a pair of Adidas sneakers. I stepped into his shoes, but they were two sizes too small, unlike everything else, which was two sizes too big.

I thought momentarily about going to the police, but I'm not ready for the questions. I don't know how efficient the cops are in Italy, but if they're looking for a murderer . . . I cut my hair and beard but not all the way. I don't want to look like the man on the book jacket.

I don't know what to do. I'm in a motel outside Pantanelle writing, writing, writing, because I have nothing else. No ideas. I'm trying to make some sense of it. I've come to the end, and tomorrow I'll write it out again because there's a clue in there somewhere. There's a reasonable answer. I just have to look harder. I'm sure. I'm sure it will come to me. If I just close my eyes and search for the moment after they dragged me away. It's there somewhere. It has to be. Otherwise . . . No. It has to be. It has to be. It has to be. God . . . where the hell is it!

Doug Devor

Doug Devor is originally from Wickliffe, Ohio just outside Cleveland. Ohio born and bred, his nomadic lifestyle has carried him all over the state, including enjoyable stops in Athens, Steubenville, Zanesville, Newark, and (currently) New Albany.

Doug is a youth director, childcare worker, cook, actor, history teacher, writer, and softball umpire. He enjoys Cleveland Indians baseball and thrice-baked potatoes.

He would like to thank Ginger Leonard for teaching him to be creative and Mindy Hotchkiss for teaching him how to focus that creativity onto a piece of paper.

Doug has written predominantly for the stage, but enjoys short fiction as well. He would write more often, but *Mass Effect 3* just came out, so that's going to take some time to get through.

THE FALL
By Doug Devor

Hard fall. Like that time Jimmy DeAngelo pushed him off the slide in second grade. Kind of like that, but harder. Where was he? White room, all white, dull light. What happened? He remembered falling, and he remembered hitting the ground, but what else? Greg sat up and examined his body for injuries. Soreness in his back, but that was normal these days. Your thirties will do that to you. Hurts your pride more than anything else. No cuts. No scratches. No bumps. Maybe a slight throbbing in his knee. Is there such a thing as a *slight* throbbing? Maybe *aching* was a better word.

Greg sat up and looked around. The empty room looked like an old warehouse with a new coat of paint. Very clean, but very old. Like his sixty-four Chevy. Great car. Died in a park. He searched his memory trying to understand how he got here, but this made him realize that his head was throbbing. It was the right word this time.

The fall. Greg looked up for answers, but saw nothing. If he had fallen to this spot, there was nowhere to fall from. The ceiling was thirty feet up—but no opening, no windows, no ledges. Even if there were, no way could he have fallen thirty feet and received only an aching knee and a throbbing head in return. No way.

He stood up. What was his last memory? Beer. He always thought it was interesting how your memory clings to tastes and smells. He was drinking a beer and sitting on his back porch. It was summer. It was Tuesday. Marissa skipped outside, slamming the screen door behind her and asked him to play dolls. He said no. Then Georgia followed and asked him to fix the gutter. He tried to say no, but that didn't work. Daughters are easier to say no to than wives.

He had fallen from the gutter. He remembered. The ladder was wet because it had just rained and he was in a hurry because he wanted to unclog the gutter and get back to his half-empty beer before it was warm. He slipped off. That was the last thing he could find in his memory. Maybe there was screaming. Maybe an ambulance? That part was fuzzy because there were only bits and pieces.

He was probably dead. The thought flooded his mind like a river, but the river was calm. Strangely calm. He didn't want to be dead, but it was odd that he seemed so at ease. He had always prided himself on his patient temperament, but he never thought it would carry with him to death.

Alone in the white warehouse. There were no lights, but there *was* light. Dim and fluorescent. He began to wander about and explore the space, as thoughts darted around his mind about heaven and hell and God and all these things you are supposed to think about when you're dead.

Greg, who fell off a ladder, was to spend eternity not in fiery torture, not in clouds of rainbows, but in an empty warehouse. Perhaps this was indicative of how he had lived his life. Loneliness set in like a lead weight on his chest.

What seemed like days, but was likely only hours had passed when he heard them. Footsteps. Not his. He turned and saw a young girl in a cherry-red dress, about the same age as Marissa, maybe younger, about six or seven. She didn't seem to notice him at first, but as he walked toward her, she looked up casually and admired him curiously. Perhaps she died, too and didn't know where she was. He didn't really care why she was there, he was just happy to see someone.

"Are you okay?" he asked.

She didn't seem interested in talking. Maybe she was in shock. He asked her again but still received no response.

"What's your name?" he persisted.

She looked boldly into his eyes. She didn't fear him like most children did. Georgia told him it was his beard that they thought was scary. When she spoke to him, it didn't seem childish. Strange.

"Do you want to play dolls?"

She looked directly at him as she spoke. Great. Not only was he dead, but now he was in a horror movie. Hopefully she wasn't an alien or a demon or something worse.

"Excuse me?"

"Do you want to play dolls?"

"Who are you?"

"Isn't that what she asked you before you fell? She asked if you wanted to play dolls?"

Hesitation. This girl wasn't a girl. And if he was dead and in heaven or hell or Buddhist heaven or whatever occurred in the afterlife, this girl wasn't here because she had died. She was something more important. Something in him said, *answer her questions.*

"Yes. I didn't play with her."

"Why not?"

"Because I didn't want to. I feel badly now."

"Do you know where you are?"

"No."

"Do you understand that you've fallen?"

"I know that I fell. Am I dead?"

"Yes, but you are not done."

"What does that mean?"

"You are dead. But you are not done."

Confusion. So he was dead, but he had already come to understand that part. His wife had asked him to fix the gutter and he died because it rained and he wanted to finish his beer. Was it his sixth or seventh? Eighth? It was funny, for all the times he had driven drunk, he had died because he had fallen off a ladder. It wasn't funny.

It was probably only nine feet. When Jimmy DeAngelo pushed him off the slide, it was probably a fifteen foot fall and he didn't have a scratch on him. So he was dead and now he was somewhere. But where he was didn't seem as important as who he was talking to. And even that didn't seem as important as what she was implying he was going to do next.

"What do you mean I'm not done?"

"You will be reborn."

Not what he expected. Was she implying that he would be re-incarnated? He never thought too much about spiritual stuff. He had gone to church, but most of the time was spent daydreaming and thinking about how he didn't want to mow the lawn when he got home. What he wouldn't give to be mowing that lawn now. He wished he paid more attention to the pastor. Maybe *he* would know what to do in this situation. Know what to say. Know what to feel. Have fewer questions. He wasn't sure which one to ask next, and was surprised the girl spoke first.

"Who are you?"

"My name is Greg Trent."

"I don't care about your name. I want to know who you are."

"I'm a law clerk."

"You define yourself by your name and your job? Is that how you want to be remembered?"

"No."

"Then who are you?"

The girl fixed her gaze on his eyes and he couldn't look away. Her stare brought a flood of thoughts that he could no longer run away from. He wanted to smell fresh cut grass after mowing his lawn. He wanted to see Marissa's smile as she played with her dolls. He wanted to feel his wife's skin on his face. He wanted to apologize to his father, he wanted to quit his job and go back to school, he wanted more. More life. If he hadn't rushed on the ladder so he could finish a beer he could have had all that. If he hadn't said no to his daughter, he could be holding her now. He would do everything differently. He wanted a second chance. He wanted more. He didn't want to leave his daughter without a father and he didn't want to leave his wife without a husband.

The girl spoke. "Do you promise?"

She knew his thoughts. He wasn't sure if he was staring into the eyes of God, or a god, or an angel. But he knew she was something more powerful than himself. With tears in his eyes he answered, "I promise."

"Who are you?"

"I'm a father. And a husband. And I want to see my family again."

The girl reached into her dress pocket and removed a crumpled flower. "Take it."

He reached for it and then jolted awake.

He had fallen asleep on his back porch. As he opened his eyes he saw his daughter wandering the back yard picking flowers. He sat up and something fell off his chest into his lap. A crumpled dandelion from his yard. His eyes filled with tears and he reached for his beer. It was half full and warm to his touch.

He put down his beer, stood up and called to his daughter.

Nate Roderick

Nate Roderick has committed himself to blurring the line between work and play; labor and leisure. His life has been enriched by a diversity of experiences that have landed him in New York City, the sea turtle inhabited beaches of Costa Rica, the summits of mountains from Georgia to Maine and the fertile fields in Connecticut and Central Ohio.

He currently works at Sunny Meadows Flower Farm in Columbus. Nate lives in Olde Towne East with his fiancée Amanda and their incredibly smart, and borderline human, dog, Bel.

"Poor Girl" was inspired by the perpetual struggle between pity, apathy and guilt he feels when confronted by a haggard soul with a desperate message scrawled on a cardboard sign.

Someday, when his body grows tired, he hopes to devote countless hours to reading the stories he's never read and writing the tales he never found time to tell.

POOR GIRL
By Nate Roderick

We deliver now! The slogan was embroidered across the
left side of my company-issued navy blue polo. Every morning I
looked in the full length mirror and shook my head. Khaki pants,
black belt, company shirt—tucked in. "It is important that our
drivers look clean, well groomed and professional." Four years of
college and all I got was this lousy polo shirt. Pathetic.

After being out of work for several months I had taken the
only job I could find—working as an independent contractor for
a local courier service. The company had a pretty good racket
going, hiring dozens of desperate saps to run God knows what God
knows where at any hour, day or night. The saps used their own
cars, and they'd pay them pennies on the dollar in commissions.
The company made a killing in delivery charges and didn't have to
worry about maintaining or repairing vehicles. I, on the other hand,
had to worry quite a bit about maintaining and repairing *my* aging
vehicle: a 1996 Honda Accord that should have been sent to the
scrap yard years ago.

I knew I had been pressing my luck, pushing her limits
by dragging her all over town, day in and day out. Lately her
age had really begun to show. Shaking and shivering, grinding
and groaning. I was driving her harder than ever, and she was
complaining at every turn. Poor girl.

Before her stint in the courier business she'd been a good
and reliable companion. We'd been everywhere together—Maine
to Montana, California to the Carolinas. I'd spent countless nights
curled up in the back seat, and her trunk had been jam-packed with
months of supplies more than a few times. She had even had a
close encounter with a small black bear once on a dark highway in
upstate New York. The bear had been hit and was spinning on its
side across the road. Boom! Boom! Her tires actually lifted off the
ground as the bear disappeared beneath us. Those were the good
old days.

There wasn't anything adventurous about being a courier car. No bears to jump or beaches to spend the night on. I was running her sometimes three or four hundred miles a day. Stops and starts. I knew she couldn't keep it up for long, but I needed her; I didn't have a choice. I would often pat her on the dash for encouragement when she rumbled too much.

"Come on, Honda," then out of guilt, "Sorry, girl."

On that particular day she had been protesting more than usual. As I turned into a gas station, an unfamiliar grinding sound came from somewhere near one of the front wheels. I rolled her up to the pump and killed the engine. My phone beeped. I snatched it from the cup holder and pressed the two-way button.

"Go ahead."

"Just checking your progress." Dispatch. Dispatch was very fond of checking your progress.

"I'm about ten minutes away. Just stopped for gas."

"Copy that. It's a firm delivery, so make sure you're there by 4:45."

"Yeah, I got it. I'll be there shortly."

"Copy that."

"Copy that," I muttered, without pressing the button.

Thirty bucks drained into the tank for the fifth time that week.

As I was pumping, I noticed a girl standing across the street on the opposite corner with her back to traffic. She was maybe twenty years old. Long blond hair. Jeans and a sweatshirt. Her head was bent down and her hands were wiping her face. Behind her on the ground was a clear plastic bag filled with clothes and a few other indiscernible items. She wiped her face several times and hung her head for an extended moment before turning around to face traffic. She was flushed, partly, I suppose, because it was forty degrees outside, and partly because she had been crying.

She was holding a folded cardboard sign with a message written in black marker. I could only see the part of the sign that was curled toward me. "REALLY NEED" was all I could make out. Just enough fingers to hold the sign were sticking out of the
40

sleeve of her sweatshirt; her other hand was tucked into her armpit. Her eyes were fixed on the ground in front of her, never looking up to meet the eyes of the oncoming drivers.

The fuel pump clicked off. I grabbed the receipt and walked around to the driver's side, still staring at the girl as I climbed in.

My phone beeped again.

"You there 905?" 905. That was me.

I slid the receipt in a manilla envelope that served as a constant reminder of how much money I was blowing on fuel, stuck the key in the ignition and gave it a crank.

Instead of firing up, or even attempting to, the sound that accompanied the turn of the key was a mere *click*. She had never done that before, but the Honda was full of surprises those days. I gave the key another twist.

Click.

"Come on girl," I said, patting the dash firmly. I tried again.

Click.

And again.

Click.

My lips tensed and I breathed out hard through my nose. I did not have time to deal with mechanical malfunctions. I needed—the car—to start.

"Come on . . ." I was pleading this time. I held my breath. Cranked.

Click.

"Shit."

The phone beeped. "905, this is Dispatch, do you copy?"

I grabbed the phone. "Yeah I copy."

"Just checking your progress. Remember that's a firm delivery."

The veteran drivers had warned me that if you ever blew a delivery, dispatch wouldn't forget it. They'd run you back and forth across town on puny, short runs that didn't pay shit. The good runs went to their favorite drivers - the ones who didn't screw up. Those were the rules. Don't blow the delivery.

"905?"

"Yeah, I'm here. I just gassed up. I'm on the way."

"Copy. Let us know when you're unloaded."

"Sure thing." I threw the phone in the cup holder. Not only could I not afford to blow the delivery, but I couldn't afford to be stranded ninety miles from home. I didn't even want to think about how much a tow would cost from there. My hand gripped the key firmly. I closed my eyes and prayed to the god of Hondas, or deliveries, or whatever.

"Please, girl, come on. I need you to start. Right—now!"
Click.

"Dammit!" I slammed my fist on the steering wheel. Droplets of sweat formed on my forehead, a heated frustration bubbling up from within. She wasn't even turning over. Not even close to starting. She'd never done anything like that before. I stepped out to get some fresh air and figure out what the hell to do.

Across the street the girl was at the driver's side of an Audi accepting a donation. The conference lasted longer than what was typical for that type of exchange. She nodded, wiping her eyes. I could see her mouth form the words "thank you."

She stepped away from the car and scampered back to her post. Traffic resumed and the line of cars streamed through the light. She was turned away again, head down, face in her hands. She was so desperate, I couldn't help but watch. For whatever reason we are obligated to gawk at tragedy. A whole race of rubberneckers.

By the time the light turned red she'd regained a minimal measure of composure and again presented her sign to the world.
REALLY NEED

It should be said that I have no soft spot for panhandlers. Living in two of the sketchier neighborhoods in Columbus for the better part of ten years had long since numbed me to their tales. I'd had them knocking on my door at eleven o'clock at night, "Hey man, I'm Mr. Johnson from down the street," shoving some stolen ID in my face. I couldn't walk three blocks without being harassed.

Several of them were permanent fixtures in the neighborhood, their presence as reliable as the street signs: there was Bumfoot, dragging his dead leg behind him until he was just around the corner. GQ, always looking sharp, glasses and a crisp haircut— his car inexplicably running out of gas parallel-parked just down down the block from wherever he happened to be standing. And Spoonman, forever feigning hunger by shoveling imaginary food into his mouth with his invisible spoon, accosting unfortunate drivers who found themselves stopped at the corner he had claimed for the day.

I'd heard every story: daughter in the hospital, stolen wallet, gotta catch the bus, bank won't cash the check, lost phone. When I was in my late teens and fresh from the suburbs I had fallen for all of their shit. My idealistic propensity for compassion had justified giving away hundreds of dollars in one and two dollar increments. But after a while my compassion withered. How many times can the same guy run out of gas on my block? If you're hungry why aren't you asking your neighbor, or sister, or cousin, or grandma, or *somebody* who would give a shit? Why did you come to this part of town without enough money to catch the bus home? I got tired of being lied to. Tired of being hassled. Fed up.

"Sorry, man," I used to say, still feeling a twinge of guilt as I walked by them with dollars in my pocket—albeit only a few. Eventually I quit saying sorry and didn't even look them in the eye.

"Hey bro, listen I—"

"No," was my curt response. Every time. Fuck you, I'd think.

Sometimes I'd really throw them for a loop by asking *them* for a dollar before they even got a word out, an exercise I found to be surprisingly satisfying.

"That's what I was gonna ask you," they'd say.

"I know."

But this girl wasn't some crackhead beggar. She didn't leave the house that morning planning on scamming whoever she could squeeze a few bucks out of. She wasn't any good at it. She couldn't even look them in the eye. If she was a real panhandler—a pro—

43

she would have been hustling up and down the line of cars, not letting anyone slip by without a shake of the head or a defensive wave of the hand. She'd be knocking on windows, pantomiming to roll it down—working it. But not her. She just stayed in her spot, avoiding eye contact with any of them, letting the sign do all the talking. A total amateur.

I wrestled my attention back to the Honda, reminding myself that I had a supposedly important package in the back that was minutes away from being late for its firm delivery. Not to mention that my beloved Honda, my only means of transportation and income generation, was dead on the spot.

You don't have to know anything about cars to know what you do when they don't start—you pull the lever, pop the hood, stick that little prop up to keep it from cracking you on the head, and stare at the engine—so that's what I did. It looked like every other engine I'd ever seen: black and silver metal, wires winding in and around and through, plastic containers filled with different colored liquids, a few colored rubber parts. None of it made much sense to me.

After that I knew what you do is jiggle stuff, so I did that too. I jiggled wires where they connect to metal. Jiggled where they connect to the battery. I jiggled everything that could be jiggled.

I found the dip-stick and checked the oil. I had a pretty strong suspicion that nothing having anything to do with the oil level would cause the car to not start, but it was the only other thing I knew how to do, so I did it. It was fine.

When my mechanical expertise was exhausted, I sat back in the driver's seat, drew in a big hopeful breath and turned the key.

Click. Surprise. I leaned my head against the headrest and considered my options. I couldn't come up with anything that didn't involve spending a lot of money I didn't have. I was screwed.

Across the street the girl's back was to the road again. She couldn't face traffic for more than one change of the light without breaking down and having to turn away. Despite my own situation,
44

I felt compelled to talk to her, to find out what the problem was. Not the *big* problem, just the immediate, paralyzing, *why are you out on the corner of the road with your bag of clothes right now* problem. Did she need a ride? I could give her a ride—well, maybe. Did she need to use a phone? How much money was she trying to scrape together to get her to whatever her next step was? It was chilly out, and she was under-dressed, she had to be cold. What was she going to do when it got dark? Surely she had somewhere to go, or someone she could call. She must have had *someone* - everyone has *someone*.

I thought of my sister, just a few years older than her. What if *she* was standing out there with that damn bag of clothes. Clear plastic. You can't judge people by looking at them, but she looked so normal. She just needed—something.

I couldn't understand why more people weren't giving her money. They just sat there in their BMWs and SUVs—glad they stopped far enough away from her that they didn't have to read her sign. Didn't have to look at her. It was the ones who got stuck right next to her that had it the hardest. They had to pretend to look down at their phones, or fidget with the kids in the back seat. Some of them did give her money, and every time she would be wiping her face, eyes down, "thank you."

After watching this go on through several changes of the light I made up my mind: I was going to go over there, talk to her, and do whatever I could do to get her off that corner. I'd give her ten bucks and take her to a restaurant. She could wait with me until I got my car running again and I'd take her wherever she needed to go. I even thought about finding a cheap hotel and putting it on my credit card.

My hand was on the car door when a bigger guy, about my age, approached her from the parking lot behind. He was eating chips and had a bottled drink tucked in his elbow. His head was cocked forward delicately. They talked. He listened and nodded while she wiped her face over and over. He said something, nodded more, kept eating his chips. They talked for two or three minutes, and he handed her a few bills. He smiled before turning and walking back to his car.

What the hell? He had taken the time to go over there, to ask what was going on, then he just walked away. If you're going to get involved you can't just leave her there, crying alone on the corner. And he didn't even give her any chips. I wondered what she could have said. What about her story made it okay for him to just nod and walk away. He gave her money—I guess that was nice, but she needed more than money. REALLY NEEDS.

My phone beeped. "905? Just checking your progress."

I resisted throwing the phone out into the road. I would've loved to watch it get crushed under a tire as someone rolled right over it. A pile of broken plastic pieces. Instead I reached into the cup holder, grasped the phone, and brought it up to my mouth.

"Yeah, I'm just a few minutes away. Traffic is a little heavy."

"Copy. Remember to call it in once you're unloaded. It's a firm delivery."

"Got it."

I tossed the phone into the passenger seat and looked back across the street. I can relate, I thought. In a month it might be me standing out there with my sign and my little bag of clothes—really needing something.

Pete! I needed Pete! He was the only guy I knew who knew anything about cars – and he knew a fair amount. He would at least have a suggestion. He had to. I pulled out my personal phone.

"Pete, glad you answered."

"Thanks."

"No, I mean, I'm in a pinch—maybe you can help."

"What's up?"

I explained to him what had happened to the Honda. He asked for all the details: how was it running before it died? What sound did it make when I tried to crank it? Did the lights work? How long did I turn the key?

"Got any ideas?"

He paused before answering, "Yeah, I've got a couple ideas,

but for your sake I hope none of them are right."

"Hm." Shit.

"Unless it's the solenoid."

"What?"

"It could be the starter solenoid."

"Yeah?"

"Maybe. Are you by yourself?"

"Yeah, but there's people around. I can get somebody."

"You'll need someone else."

A glimmer of hope.

"What do I need to do?"

Pete explained that the solenoid was part of the starter, and I could find it by following the large cable from the positive side of the battery. Even I could do that. He said it was silver and mostly cylindrical. If I could get someone to bang on the starter with a screwdriver while I kept turning the key, there was a chance—a small chance - that it would fire up. It was my best shot.

"Pete, you're a lifesaver." I hung up.

When I got out of the car to find an accomplice there was a woman talking to the girl. She was listening intently. The girl was crying. The woman looked like she was old enough to be her mom. Her motherly instincts were probably kicking in and she would have no choice but to help her. She'd have to. She'd take the girl back to her house and let her sleep there for the night, or take her somewhere safe. She'd make sure she was all right. There was no way she would leave her standing there.

It was getting into rush hour so there was a lot of traffic in and out of the gas station. I spotted a guy wearing Carhartts and a baseball cap stepping out of a pickup truck. *My assistant.* I approached him and explained the situation. He was somewhat skeptical of the plan, but he was willing to help.

"Do you have a screwdriver or something we could use to tap on it?" I asked.

"I got a hammer."

A little heavy, but it would do.

The guy didn't need any guidance finding the starter. I got in and he started tapping with the hammer. I turned the key.

Click. Click. Click. Click. Click.

"Keep going!" I shouted. "Come on, Honda . . . come on . . . " My teeth were clenched. I kept turning.

Click. Click. Click.

Then again.

Click. Click.

"Come on . . . "

And again.

She started.

"Yes! YES!" I banged with my open hand on the dash. "That a girl, Honda. Thank you. Thank you!"

"I'll be damned. I'd say you got mighty lucky," the guy said as I dropped the hood.

"Thanks man. I really appreciate it."

"No problem. Good luck." He headed back to his truck.

Across the street the woman was gone, but the girl was still standing on the corner. Two people had gone out of their way to talk to her, heard what she had to say, and they hadn't helped. I wanted to know her story. She must have had a good reason for deciding that her best option was to just keep standing there with her sign and her bag of clothes. I wished she would stop crying.

As much as I wanted to go talk to her I felt uneasy about making her explain herself to another stranger. Her life wasn't some sort of spectacle for everyone to take turns looking at. She was embarrassed enough as it was. I didn't want to be sticking my nose where it didn't belong just to make me feel like I had tried to do the right thing. Maybe when I drove up next to her something would strike me. Either way, I had a delivery to make, and neither of us were getting any closer to what we needed as long as I stood there staring across the street.

I got back in the car and finally pulled out of the station, taking my place in the line of cars approaching her corner. I was just two cars back when the light turned red and we all came to a stop. My phone was beeping constantly.

"905? 905? Do you copy? We need to know if you're unloaded."

The car that was stopped next to her called her over. Again there was the drawn out exchange, complete with the nodding and tears. A feminine hand reached out the window and she grasped it with both hands, nodding hard as if she were agreeing to something. One of her hands pulled away to wipe her face. She stepped back onto the grass, keeping her back to the cars as she tried to regain control of herself. Her sign dropped to the ground.

I heard beeping and something about "real time updates," and the number 905 repeated over and over.

Her face was being rubbed raw by the sleeves of her dampened sweatshirt. She bent down to pick up her sign, lifted her head, took a deep breath, and turned around.

LEFT BY HUSBAND
REALLY FAR FROM FAMILY
NEED MEDICINE. HAVE TO GET
HOME. PLEASE HELP

Someone in the world had actually found it acceptable to leave her there. To discard her, leave her helpless, without so many of the things that she needed to survive. Her ability to preserve her own well being had been ripped away from her. She had been chewed up and spit out on that corner.

If her problems were easy to solve one of the two helpful strangers would have done it. That was why they had talked to her—because they wanted to help, but there was only so much they could do. She was far from where she needed to be. Far from her family. From her medicine. A bus ride to somewhere far away could be hundreds of dollars—more than even the most generous soul would fork over to a stranger standing on a corner. A few dollars, sure. Ten or twenty even. But what she needed was more than any one of us could give her.

49

I said something like a prayer, not to the god of Hondas or deliveries, but to the god that helps poor broken girls get off the corner so they have somewhere safe to sleep at night. I asked him to please work a little of his magic for this girl. Help her to stop crying. Help her get what she really needs—get her home. Make her well.

I pulled the last five bucks out of my wallet and rolled it up to make for an easy hand-off. She was holding her sign and staring blankly at the ground in front of her when the light turned green. She turned away as the line of cars started to move.

When I got up next to her I stopped. The car behind me laid on the horn. She turned around.

"Hey! Here—" I said, holding the money out the window.

The horn blew again.

She shook her head and motioned for me to go.

"Here. Take it. Please."

She was sill shaking her head as she stepped up and grabbed the cash.

"He must be a jerk. You deserve better. I wish I could help."

"Thank you," she said. Tears were streaming down her face. "Go. Go!"

"I'm sorry." I didn't know what else to say.

She jumped out of the road as the car behind me blasted the horn emphatically. I held my middle finger up where I knew the driver would be able to see it clearly and accelerated into the intersection. I looked over my shoulder as I turned. She was facing away from the road, head hanging.

I ignored the repeated calls from dispatch on my way to the delivery address, using the time in transit to accept that it was going to be shit runs for me for the foreseeable future. Not only had I blown the delivery, but I had blown it spectacularly—and done a heck of a job at pissing off dispatch in the process.

The building was dark as I rolled into the parking lot. It was 5:23. The door was locked and no one answered when I rang the service bell. I deposited the cargo in a somewhat discrete spot behind a bush next to the main entrance. No signature.

I hit the two-way button on my phone.

"Dispatch, this is 905. I'm unloaded."

"Where the hell have you been? You were supposed to be there more than a half hour ago. We've been trying to—"

"I hit traffic, and my phone—I couldn't ... service was bad ... it was—sorry."

"This is not going to reflect well on your reliability as a driver. Our client is going to be furious! What are we supposed to tell them? That your phone didn't have service? That you hit traffic?"

"I had trouble getting out of the gas station and . . . never mind. Sorry."

"Report to the office at 8:00 a.m. sharp tomorrow morning. We're going to need you to sign off on this delivery and review the contractor agreement. Do you copy?"

Once I was back inside the Honda I instructed my GPS to show me the way home.

"905. Do you copy?"

I held down the button with the little red telephone on it. Blue streaks swirled around the word "Goodbye" before the screen went black.

The Honda ran as smoothly as she had in months on the way home. Maybe the god of Hondas had heard my prayer after all and was providing us both safe passage that night. Or maybe I was being rewarded, in the smallest and most subtle way, for trying to do something good when it would have been just as easy to do nothing. I couldn't get the image of the girl crying on the corner out of my head. I imagined she was still standing there. I didn't get her off the corner, but at least I helped. The Honda shivered as we exited the interstate, reminding me that she was never going to run like she did when she was young, but I had gotten her going, and we were both going to make it home okay.

Two blocks from my house I was stopped at the light at the intersection of Kelton and Main. A man in a shabby black trench coat and an ancient L.A. Lakers hat was at the window of the car in front of me. It was Spoonman, his hand following the never ending circular path from a nonexistent bowl to his mouth.

Any second he would be turning his attention to me, the next faceless driver in the endless flow of featureless cars drifting through his existence that night. If it had been any other day, I would have waved him off, or ignored him altogether. But it wasn't. That day the world had it out for all of us. All the people who already had it hard had to have it just a little harder—me, the girl, maybe even Spoonman—and there wasn't a damn thing any of us could do about it. At least not on our own. I had needed Pete and the guy in the Carhartt's. The girl on the corner had needed all of us, everyone who was willing to reach out to her in one way or another. Any normal day I wouldn't have even looked in Spoonman's direction, but that day I was on his side, and I decided to test his story once and for all. Maybe, just maybe he really was hungry, and didn't have any other way of going about it. Maybe he did need something that day. Maybe he needed—me.

My unfinished lunch was sitting in the passenger seat: a plastic bag with a banana, half an egg salad sandwich and some Wheat Thins. My plan had been to finish the meal, wash it down with a glass of chocolate milk and call it dinner, but maybe he needed it more than me. At least I had somewhere to sleep, someone to call if times got really tough.

I rolled down the window and motioned him over. He hustled toward me, shuffling his feet. I'd never paid enough attention to notice how filthy his coat was or that his shoes didn't have any laces. He was a disaster. When he got to my car, I grabbed the plastic bag and held it out the window. An offering of sorts.

"Can I get a dollar?" he said.

The food was hanging over the black asphalt of Kelton Avenue, inches from the stains on his shirt. I shoved it out a little further.

"Can I get a dollar, man? Please?"

The light turned green. I let the bag hang a second longer

before retracting the offering and looking up at his face. My eyes tightened the slightest bit as they locked with his.

"That's what I was going to ask you."

He cocked his head and wrinkled his brow as he tried to understand what I was saying. I pressed the metal button to roll up the window and tossed the grub in the passenger seat.

As I crossed Main St. I watched in the rear-view mirror as Spoonman stepped up to the first car stopped going the other way. His usual charade was in full effect. A well-intentioned sucker cracked his window a couple inches and slipped a dollar out, which Spoonman greedily tucked in his pocket with one hand while he shoveled food with his imaginary spoon at the next car in line.

That's how you do it, I thought. A real pro.

Deborah Cheever Cottle

Deborah Cottle was born in Newfoundland, Canada and grew up in rural Indiana where she learned to entertain herself by exploring nature, making up her own games, and reading voraciously. She also loved to write her own stories and dreamed of the day she would see one of her stories in a real book.

Sticking to her Indiana roots, Deborah attended Purdue University and received a B.A. in Education and an M.S. in Counseling. She then began a career in education that included serving as a middle school guidance counselor, an elementary teacher and a reading specialist. She especially enjoys helping young students develop their own literacy skills.

Deborah and her husband, David, have lived in Westerville, Ohio for the past twenty-six years. They enjoy taking frequent cross-country road trips to visit their son, Aaron, who lives and works in Seattle.

As a recent retiree, Deborah has put her writing ambitions back on the front burner. "The Ant Doctor" is her first published story. She is also exploring publishing options for a completed mystery novel.

Deborah would like to thank her husband for his unfailing support and encouragement. She also thanks Columbus Creative Cooperative for helping to make her dream come true.

THE ANT DOCTOR

By Deborah Cheever Cottle

Noontime sun beat down upon the cluster of young boys. Sweat washed salty trails over their faces and glistened on the shoulders of those boys whose mothers allowed them to go shirtless.

"Here comes another one," a thin voice yelled, and the group looked in unison towards the spot where he pointed. A large black ant trudged across the hot concrete, moving unknowingly through a maze of deadly feet. A big boy, clearly years older than the rest, stepped towards the ant. Frank Fenway raised a tennis-shoed foot over the unsuspecting creature and held the pose for dramatic effect. Then slowly, inch-by-inch, he lowered the foot, casting a giant shadow across the ant's path.

The circle of young bodies drew closer as the foot neared the pavement. Then in one quick movement it was down. Frank's eyes, black as the blackest ant, blazed as he pinned the small body with his toe, imagining he could feel it crushing like a sugar cube beneath his foot. But that, he knew, was only his imagination. Secretly, he cushioned the blow with his heel so that his weight was never really on the insect. Not enough to crush—only to cripple.

An expectant hush fell over the group as Frank pulled his foot back, revealing a motionless black ball. He dropped quickly to his knees, adjusting his position so that the sun would not throw a shadow across his stage. It was important that everyone clearly see the good deed he was about to perform.

In fevered tones, the boys unleashed an eerie chant into the stifling air. "Ant Doctor, Ant Doctor, do your tricks."

Frank felt the flow of their voices wash over him like a refreshing breeze. He drew strength from their words—words that he had planted like tiny seeds in their minds. With a serious smile, he flashed the dark coals of his eyes around the reverent group and pulled a small twig from his back pocket. Gently he began to probe the small body, causing the ant to marshal its strength, to fight for its life against this new attack.

As he prodded, the ant began to uncoil, dragging its body in drunken circles as it tried to escape. Frank continued to push at it until slowly, the ant regained its sense of direction. It began to walk a nearly straight line, dragging its rear end slightly as it beat a path for the shelter of the grass. He chased it with the stick, touching it

55

slightly from time to time just so it wouldn't decide to stop and ruin the effect.

A murmur of awed appreciation rose from the boys as the ant reached the end of the concrete and became lost among the yellow-green blades of grass. Once again Frank Fenway—"The Ant Doctor", as the younger boys in the neighborhood called him—had worked his miracle.

Frank rocked back on his heels and then slowly stood up. He felt a warm stir of satisfaction as he looked down into the shining, eager eyes that rose to meet his.

Once again he let his gaze sweep his audience. "Who wants to try next?" he asked, cleverly turning the mocking undercurrent into a friendly inquiry. The boys stood quietly, each afraid they would appear a great failure in the afterglow of Frank's miraculous feats.

"Don't be afraid. It doesn't hurt to try. How about you, Tommy? Come over here and I'll help you."

Tommy Turnic felt his face flush with pride. Frank had picked him—and even better, he had called him by name.

Tommy threw a smug look towards the other boys as he walked towards Frank. They wouldn't dare call him Tommy Turnip now. Not with Frank there. Not with Frank as his friend.

"Okay. There's one coming now," Frank said as he took Tommy by the shoulders and pointed him in the right direction. Tommy watched as the black dot grew closer. He walked slowly towards it and felt a tangible push of heat as the other boys closed around him.

He raised his foot over the ant, leaving it suspended in the air as he tried to duplicate Frank's actions. Slowly he eased it down until he could feel the sidewalk against his shoe and he knew, with a sinking feeling in his stomach, that he had made an ant pancake.

"That's right. Stomp it hard," Frank coached, and without the knowledge of the secret heel hold, Tommy ground his foot against the pavement.

"Okay. Let's see what we've got." Once again Frank laid his hand on Tommy's shoulder. The feeling was good, comforting, but still Tommy hesitated. What if he lifted his foot and the ant was gone? What if it was stuck to the bottom of his shoe and he had to scrape it off like a wad of gum? What if the boys laughed at him? What if *Frank* laughed at him? Slowly he tilted his foot away, leaning forward to see what lay beneath. He breathed a sigh of relief. The ant was still there—a bumpy, black streak on the pavement.

"Okay, I'm going to let you use my special tool," Frank said and Tommy felt sure he felt a surge of power as he took the twig from Frank's fingers.

He dropped to the ground and began to poke at the remains. A piece of ant broke off and stuck to the stick. A loud burst of laughter chiseled through Tommy's heart, but stopped abruptly. Tommy glanced up and saw that Frank was staring at the perpetrator with eyes of ice.

"Let him concentrate. He's doing fine." Frank's words were strong and steady and Tommy felt a fresh surge of hope charge into his body. He began poking at the dot again, trying to stir it into action.

"I think it moved. Yes, it definitely moved a little," Frank said and the boys murmured in agreement.

Tommy hadn't seen it move, but if Frank said it had, it must be so. He pushed at the ant again and again, but it was no use. This ant just wasn't going to get up and march away.

"I think that's enough for now," Frank said finally. "It was a real good first time. You made it move a little and not everyone can do that. I think he deserves a round of applause, don't you guys?"

Obediently, the boys smashed their hands together. Tommy felt his chest swell with happiness as he stood up nonchalantly and brushed his hands on the seat of his pants. He looked towards Frank for further approval. Frank caught his gaze and clamped on to it with his own.

"Maybe someday, kid, you'll even be as good as me."

Tommy tried to smile. The words were surely meant as a compliment. But there was something in Frank's eyes that went beyond words—something cold and dark that seemed to carry a secret message shared just by the two of them. A message that said, "You're not the Ant Doctor, kid. You're not as good as me and don't ever forget it."

Frank smiled inwardly as he saw the hurt in Tommy's eyes and welcomed the heady rush of power that followed—the power of the Ant Doctor.

Jenny L. Maxey

Jenny L. Maxey is originally from Morgantown, West Virginia. She earned her Bachelor's Degree in Political Science, Masters of Public Administration, and Juris Doctor from West Virginia University. Although writing was never the forefront of her education, it has never drifted from her educational requirements and personal interests.

Jenny's historical-fiction short, "Ladybug," collides her newcomer status in Columbus, Ohio with her fondness for and experience in politics. Jenny would like to thank the Columbus Creative Cooperative writing workshoppers for their critiques of the first few drafts, as well as her dear friend Jessica for taking interest in the very first attempt at this story. Jenny specifically thanks her husband, Doug, for his unconditional support and encouragement in this venture.

This is Jenny's first ever fictional story. She has previously been published in the *West Virginia Law Review* for her article entitled: "A Myriad of Misunderstanding Standing: Decoding Judicial Review for Gene Patents."

Presently, Jenny is working on a non-fiction book to assist prospective law students with saving money before, during, and after law school.

LADYBUG
By Jenny L. Maxey

Evelyn Burnett stood at the bottom of the stairs and yelled. "Ladybuuuuuuug! Come quick! There's something you need to watch on TV!"

"What is it, Mom? I'm workin' on somethin'!" Colleen rolled her light brown eyes. Ladybug wasn't her favorite nickname, but like most nicknames, once one person plants it into the minds of others, it grows like a stubborn weed and is tough to yank out. Her mother made it up for her when she was a little girl, since Colleen was always intent on getting her way: "Quit bugging me, Ladybug," she'd say. Even now that she wasn't a little girl who could manipulate her parents with a few bats of her eyelashes, she still managed to charm her prey into doing what she wanted them to do most of the time.

Colleen turned down the radio and held up the poster board she was working on. It was lime green and in big, black letters read "DRESS CODES GOTTA GO!" Around the lettering, she drew a few peace signs to fill up some of the empty space.

"Perfect." She set the poster aside, yanked her copper colored hair into a high ponytail, and rushed down the stairs. She walked into the family room, where her parents and younger brother, Casey, gathered around the television. Her father, Walt, stood with his arms folded across his chest and was shaking his head in disapproval. Her mother sat on the arm of the sofa with her hand cupped over her mouth. Colleen sneaked up behind Casey, who was sitting cross-legged on the floor, and tickled at his ribs. He let out a soft giggle, but didn't take his eyes from the television.

"What's going on, Mom?"

"It's that college you want to go to—Kent State. I knew all this protesting would cause trouble eventually."

Before Colleen could respond, the television interrupted: "Four students have been killed and nine others are wounded after the Ohio National Guard fired shots to break up a protest," the news anchor announced. Hovering over his shoulder, a black and white photograph depicted a young man lying face down on the pavement, with a young woman kneeling over him. Her arms were raised toward the sky in a plea for help and she was screaming with tears in her eyes.

"That's crazy," Colleen whispered. She had never seen an image this graphic on television before. Then, the report showed the school pictures of the four dead.

"After President Nixon announced last Thursday that the nation would invade Cambodia, some of the Kent State student body began a sequence of demonstrations," the anchorman continued. "University officials learned that a protest was scheduled for this afternoon and requested that students cease all demonstration plans. Most students abandoned the area when the National Guard released containers of tear gas; however, the Guard continued to advance and began shooting. Investigations concerning today's events are ongoing."

Colleen sat in stunned silence. The anchorman's words turned into muffled babble, as if her head was suddenly under water. She couldn't remember anything of this magnitude ever happening before, especially so close to home. Her mother's outburst suddenly awakened her from her trance.

"Okay, that's enough!" Evelyn said as she stood to turn off the television. "You are *done* with the protests, Ladybug. No protests and no Kent State!"

"What! Why are you turning this on *me*?"

"It's for your own good. These demonstrations aren't for sweet girls like you. That could've been you!"

"But—"

"No 'buts.' I shouldn't have let you convince me that going away to school was a good idea in the first place . . . especially Kent State. That school is too—it's too politically charged."

"Dad, she's crazy! Tell her!" Colleen looked desperately at her father.

"Now calm down, Evelyn. This was a tragic accident," Walt said. "Maybe she can go to a local college instead. Something close to home and a little less 'out there' politically."

"And no more protests!" Evelyn added.

Colleen took in a deep breath and forced a sugary smile toward her parents. It was best to pull out the Ladybug strategy for now and play nice. "Okay, Mom. Can we talk about where I'm going to college later? We should be thinking about what's just happened and reflect. Actually, I think I'll reflect on this in my room." Without another word, Colleen darted up the stairs.

She rummaged through her room, stuffing a toothbrush, comb, and a few other necessities into her backpack. "I can't believe her. She knows I've wanted to go to Kent State for years." Slowly, Colleen pushed open her window. She slung the backpack over her arm and carefully climbed down the trellis under her window.

As Colleen rode her bike to her best friend Karen's house, the images from the news kept flashing in her mind. Surely, her mother was overreacting and the events of today were just a fluke. One thing was for sure, there was no chance she was going to stay in her hometown for college. It would be no more than a continuation of high school—the same people, the same hangouts, and constant parental supervision.

Karen answered the door, her eyebrows lifted in surprise to see Colleen standing there.

"Hey, Ladybug! What'cha doin' here?"

"I needed to get away from my mom for a little bit. Mind if I stay the night?"

"Of course! Come in! Did you see the news?"

"Yeah, crazy isn't it?"

"My sister called from her dorm to let us know she's okay. She's on her way home now."

"Did the campus close?"

"Yeah, but she said that the students are doing a walk-out on campuses all over the state in support of the victims. Some of them are going to the Capitol building tomorrow to protest."

"What a great idea …" Colleen's mind reeled. "We should go too!" The only protests she had been a part of before were at her high school. Plus, this would be a great opportunity to prove to her mother that protests could be safe and that she could be on her own.

"I don't know . . . protests aren't really my thing. I just want to stay out of it." Karen said.

"Oh c'mon. Don't be such a chicken. This will be good for you! Think about it. You could get on the news, and then maybe Bobby Miller will finally call you up."

"Ew, Bobby Miller? Uh, no thanks! I'm so over him."

"Fine, whatever." *I have to do this*, she thought, *even if I go alone.*

Sunlight streamed through Karen's uncovered window and awakened Colleen from a light, fitful sleep. Karen lent her an ivory V-neck sweater with pale, pink flowers embroidered along the neckline and a pair of dusty-rose-colored corduroys that flared below the knee. She evaluated herself in the mirror. The pale flowers complemented her peaches-and-cream complexion. Colleen didn't want to overdo it with make-up so she only wore a little mascara and smudged her lips with a tinted balm.

Fifteen minutes later, Colleen climbed the narrow city bus steps. It was a twenty minute ride from her home in the suburbs to downtown Columbus. She rested her forehead on the glass window, and let the musty fumes and the hum of the bus's engine lull her into a trance. She rehearsed her introductory sentence over and over again in her head. It was a beautiful spring day, and today the streams of sunlight would be her spotlight.

When she arrived at the Capitol, the courtyard was bare. The walls of the building stood tall, and were made of cold, strong stone. She wondered if maybe she was too early. In the distance, she saw a tall man walking towards the building. He was dressed in a navy suit and carried a brief case. He looked important, so she decided to follow him.

Inside, the building was a labyrinth of limestone. Colleen watched as the man meandered down the hallways where the walls were splashed with shades of agriculture—sky blues and straw yellows, with doors the color of shaded grass. Colleen pressed her

62

back against the wall as the man stepped around a corner and into an office.

"Good morning, Senator Reiling," she heard a staffer say.

"Don't you watch the news, Henry? What's so good about it?"

Henry did not respond. After a moment, he changed the subject, "Your first appointment is in an hour. I've also got three bills for you to look at. The Senate President wants you to co-sponsor one of them."

"Cancel my appointment, and tell the Senate President to go find someone else to co-sponsor. That bill is ludicrous. It won't make a damn difference …"

Henry walked out of the office without responding and turned a corner, disappearing down the hall. Colleen edged closer to peer into the crack of the Senator's door.

"Fools. Always trying to implement stricter gun laws. Criminals don't follow gun laws," the Senator grumbled to no one in particular. He lumbered over to his large, oak desk and hunched over the bills Henry had laid out for him, allowing his gold-rimmed glasses to slide to the tip of his nose as he read.

The office door gave a long creak as it opened. The Senator looked up in surprise as Colleen stumbled inside.

"Hello, Senator Reiling. My name is Ladybug … I mean Colleen Burnett." She held out her hand to shake the Senator's, but then she dropped her arm and did an awkward curtsy. "I'm here because I want to know your take on the Kent State shootings. What will you do to protect our freedom of speech if further rallies form on college campuses?" She rolled off in one breath.

The Senator chuckled to himself. "Please sit … you said Colleen, right? Or do you want to be called Ladybug?"

"It's Colleen. Ladybug's a nickname. I don't know why I mentioned it."

"It seems you watched the news last night."

She nodded. "I watch the news often, sir. I also participate in demonstrations at my school all the time, and I want to be safe when I do it."

"Hear that, Henry? At least someone besides me watches the news!" He shouted over Colleen's head. "I can see how the events from yesterday could cause concern for you, Colleen." He paused, then proceeded politely. "Speaking of school, shouldn't you be there right now?"

"No offense sir, but it seems like you're avoiding my question."

"Goodness you're persistent! As you probably know, Colleen, investigations have aleady begun and will be ongoing. Until we know more, it's difficult to move forward. The Constitution already protects the freedom of speech and the freedom to peaceably assemble. The investigation will determine whether the demonstration was peaceful and, if it was, then the actions of the guard will be examined. I don't think there's anything more I can do."

A look of confusion and disappointment crossed Colleen's face. The Senator glanced out the window, where a large gathering was beginning to form in front of the building. "Well, Colleen, if you're here to demonstrate, I think your opportunity has arisen outside on the lawn. Would you like to walk out there and see what's going on?"

Colleen's face lit up. "Yes, definitely!"

The Senator and Colleen rushed toward the commotion outside. The chants grew louder as they came closer to the entrance of the building. People walking along the sidewalks stopped to hear the announcements. There were roughly fifty college-aged students gathered on the Capitol lawn. Several people were chanting, "WHEN YOU THREATEN WITH GUNS, WE HAVE NO AMENDMENT ONE!"

Some of the protestors were staggered on the steps in front of the Capitol, using it as an impromptu stage. A young man who stood on the highest step was talking about the Kent State shootings. He seemed to be the organizer of the group.

"Students were peaceably gathered on the Kent State University campus. Their voices were smothered in gas and silenced by gunfire. They retreated and yet the guard continued to advance." The man stated his words in a cadence; like a verse, with the chants in the background added as a chorus.

64

Colleen looked up at the Senator. "Do you think I could jump in with the chanters?" Her voice quivered.

"Sure. Go enjoy yourself. Show us curmudgeons how to make a difference!" The Senator smiled at her. He watched as Colleen jumped in with the crowd of chanters on the steps.

Just as he turned to go back into his office, someone yelled, "He's got a gun!" The protest organizer was waving a gun above his head and yelled something like "guns need to be destroyed or America will be destroyed."

The man pulled the trigger, and a shot burst into the sky. Chaos quickly erupted in the courtyard of the Capitol. The onlookers scrambled away and the protestors shoved each other to get away from the man with the loaded gun. The scene unraveled in slow motion for the Senator. He saw one of the protestors fall backward into the armed man. As the man tumbled downward, his finger tightened around the trigger. The gun let off a shot in the direction of Colleen.

Capitol security grabbed the Senator by his armpits and dragged him inside. Walkie-talkies sounded off that a gun had fired two shots. More officers ran past; their hands reaching for their holsters.

"Unhand me right now!" The Senator struggled to release himself from their grasp. Once he finally pulled away, he threw open the doors and bolted outside. Sounds of screaming and gunshots filled the air. His eyes darted around the area, sorting out the mass hysteria.

Then, his eyes stopped, and his heart. There, slumped over several steps, was Colleen. Her copper-red hair was matted with a brighter shade of red. The Senator ran over to her and scooped her small body up in his arms. Her eyes were closed and her face was already lifeless. He cradled her body close to his as he ran back into the Capitol.

The building seemed so large and unfamiliar as it blurred around him. His heavy feet clapped emptily against the marble floors. He tried several doors, but they were locked. He ran, searching for anyone to help him. The Senator stopped in the center of the rotunda.

No one was nearby. He knelt and gently laid Colleen against the cool floor.

"Help! Someone please, help! Please!" The Senator cried. But his pleas went unanswered.

Months had passed since Colleen's death. The brisk autumn breeze sent a shiver through the Burnett house. Leaves of gold and copper were woven between the branches, imitating her hair in the sunlight. Three soft knocks at the door interrupted the silence. Casey opened the door to see a tall, broad-shouldered man peering at him over his gold-framed glasses. He wore a sturdy gray suit, mostly hidden by an unbuttoned, camel-hair overcoat.

"Is this the Burnett residence?" asked the man.

Evelyn appeared behind Casey at the doorway. "Yes," she replied. Her eyebrows were drawn together. Then, a wave of recognition washed over her face. "Why, Senator Reiling, what brings you here today?" She smoothed out her dress and her fingers fluttered to her hair.

"May I come in? I'd like to discuss something with you and your family."

"Of course, please come in."

"Walt," she called over her shoulder, "Senator Reiling is here."

Everyone settled into the family room. "Mr. Senator, can I get you anything? Tea? Coffee?" asked Evelyn.

"No, no thank you. I don't wish to impose any more than I have already. I've come to offer my condolences for your loss."

"Well, it took you a while." Walt muttered.

"What my husband means . . . " Evelyn gave her husband a sideways glance, ". . . is that the medical team told us you stayed with her until they arrived and that you kept saying it was your fault for some reason. They said you tried your best to help our Ladybug."

"I know, and I hope you can accept my apologies for my delay in speaking with you all firsthand," he paused, and met Walt's eyes. "But it really was my fault. She asked my permission to participate in the protest. I shouldn't have encouraged her to go. I don't know

66

what I was thinking. It was completely irresponsible."

"Well, if you'd gotten to know Ladybug better, you would've known she loved any kind of protest. She would likely have gotten wrapped up in that protest whether you encouraged her or not," Evelyn said almost proudly.

"I wanted to let you know that your daughter . . . she . . . she changed my life that day. She reminded me of myself at that age. Her enthusiasm . . . I guess it was something I had left behind in my youth. Over time, the politics got to me. It took these past few months for me to figure this all out. I will always be grateful to her."

"Well I'm glad our daughter had a positive effect on you, but I still don't understand why you're here," Walt said.

The Senator cleared his throat. "With your permission, I would like to honor Colleen with the following resolution." He gently slid a sheet of paper across the coffee table. "I tried to think of a way for every Ohioan to know about your daughter; a way that could recognize her ambitious nature. I believe if it is done in this manner, she can live on in Ohio's memory for eternity."

The paper had "DRAFT" printed in large letters at the top and "RESOLUTION TO ADOPT THE LADYBUG AS OHIO'S STATE INSECT" underneath. It read:

The ladybug is symbolic of the people of Ohio – she is proud and friendly, bringing delight to millions of children when she alights on their hand or arm to display her multi-colored wings, and she is extremely industrious and hardy, able to live under the most adverse conditions and yet retain her beauty and charm, while at the same time being of inestimable value to nature.

Evelyn looked at the Senator with tears shimmering in her eyes, "Mr. Senator, this sounds just like *our* Ladybug."

Tina Higgins

Tina is living life slightly out of order.

After graduating from Mt. Gilead High School (Ohio), she started a career in the Air Force. Twenty years of aircraft maintenance and multiple desert visits later, she retired. She and her family moved back to Ohio where she enrolled in The Ohio State University, and obtained a B.A. in English with a minor in Popular Culture.

Currently she is trying to figure out what she wants to be when she grows up.

What she does know is that she is grateful to her friends and family for putting up with her crazy life. Props go to her mother Carla, and daughter Allie, for being her personal editorial staff; her daughters, Katie and Dani, for taking care of things when mom is writing; her husband David for keeping it all together. Much of this story is about them.

As for future projects, Tina is always looking for others with whom to collaborate. She would love to receive your email at TinasSharedWorld@gmail.com.

13 HOURS
By Tina Higgins

00:00

It wasn't an explosion. One minute they were in the air, the next in the water. The details were never clear to Lisa. Things just went wrong. An oxygen mask hit Lisa in the head, awakening her. The other people on the plane were yelling, and the flight attendants were trying to get everyone to calm down and assume the crash position. She looked up at her mom, who was pale but trying to put on a brave face. Lisa realized that on the other side of her mom she could see sky. Was that right? Should see be able to see clouds? What happened to the overhead compartment?

Suddenly, everything was wet, and Lisa's dark blond hair was floating up around her face. She felt like one of those diving rings her parents threw into the backyard pool, sinking to the bottom. The kids would race to be the first to dive in, get it, and bring it back to the surface, while her parents cheered them on. Only there was nothing exciting or fun about this.

Lisa, weighted down by the seat belt, was pulled down deeper into the water. Then she felt the seatbelt loosen. There were hands pulling her out of her seat and pushing her up. Lisa started swimming. It wasn't a thought, but a response, an automatic reaction to things her brain hadn't yet begun to understand.

00:15

Lisa's head broke the surface of the water. Her hair covered her eyes, and ocean water splashed into her mouth. It was warm and salty, just like at the beach. She remembered her dad telling her not to swallow it because it would make her throw up. But this water wasn't close to the beach, and her dad wasn't there to pick her up and carry her back to the blanket.

She yelled for help. She called for her mother. She screamed.

She started to swim but realized that she had no idea which way to go. Surrounded by debris from the aircraft Lisa noticed something that looked like a seat from the airplane. She grabbed it and looked around for something else to hang onto. She just floated.

00:45

Several pieces of the airplane floated to the surface, one of them large enough for Lisa to crawl onto. When she first tried, she felt the worst pain she'd ever had in her left arm. She looked at her arm and saw that it was black and blue, and twice the size of her right arm. She tried again and her arm gave out—it was just too painful. She rested a few minutes and tried one more time, screaming in pain, and she made it. She laid her head on the seat as tears ran down her face.

Smaller pieces of the plane, luggage, and debris made their way to the surface. There were other things; things Lisa didn't want to look too closely at. She looked away and tried not to think of them. She thought she saw a bag a man in the next row was trying to stuff into the overhead compartment. She cried quietly to herself and prayed that it was all a dream. The waves gently rocked her and Lisa began to drift off to sleep. She felt a strange sensation of safety, like being a baby rocked to sleep in her mother's arms.

01:45

Lisa looked up at the sky to watch the clouds go by. When she was just a kid, three, maybe four, her older brother used to tell her stories about the things he saw in the clouds. There were dragons that he would slay for her, evil wizards to defeat. Sometimes Mickey Mouse would stop by to see her, but mostly there was some kind of trouble that only her big brother could solve. A tree limb could be a sword or a machine gun. He was always there to rescue her.

Something in the clouds caught Lisa's eye. It was a plane. It

70

circled around the area a few times. Maybe it saw her. She sat up straight and waved her right arm wildly. She couldn't tell if they saw her. They circled the area a couple of more times and left.

05:26

Lisa didn't know what time it was, but was sure it was almost dinnertime. Her stomach was growling. She hadn't had anything to eat since the cinnamon roll her mom bought her in the airport. The sun was going down fast. Lisa thought it would be funny if the sun sizzled as it sank into the ocean. It would sound like the hamburgers her father grilled in the summer.

Dad would spend all day getting things ready. He would run to the store and get a big bag of charcoal, lighter fluid, hamburgers. hot dogs, soda, and chips. He would go outside, arrange the charcoals in little pyramids, and soak them with lighter fluid. He would tell Mom how charcoal made food taste better than gas grills. Yes, gas was quick but charcoal was much, much better. Mom would turn to the kids and wink. Dad gave the same speech every time he grilled. Sometimes Mom would help him give the speech, and sometimes she would argue with him, just to get him wound up. The kids would all giggle.

Dad put the match to the charcoal and it burst into flames. He threw his arms up and looked at the sky and yelled, "I have created fire! MAWAHAHAHA!" Then he would make caveman noises that would have the kids rolling on the ground laughing.

07:37

There were more stars out there than Lisa had seen in her whole life. Lisa tried to count them, but there were just too many. She recognized some of the constellations, like Orion and the Big Dipper. She learned about them in school in sixth grade. Her dad taught her that stars twinkle and planets don't.

10:13

The air temperature had dropped drastically when the sun
went down. It became hard to breath. It took every ounce of energy
Lisa had just to keep her eyes open. She couldn't focus her mind
on anything. Her skin was red from the sun and wind. Her hair
was stiff with salt. She was so thirsty and hungry, and her stomach
hurt. She was getting weaker and weaker. She was having trouble
maintaining her balance on her makeshift raft. She almost didn't
notice the pain in her arm anymore. Giving up was just easier.

13:00

The boat's searchlight landed on the body of a young girl
with long, dark blond hair. She didn't answer their calls. Someone
jumped into the water, holding on to a lifesaver tied to a rope. He
swam out to her, put the lifesaver around her, and swam her back
to the boat, where others had lowered a basket. The swimmer laid
her on it and belted her in so she wouldn't fall. They pulled her up
then checked for a pulse and for breathing. When they couldn't find
either, they started CPR. Everyone kept talking to her, asking her to
come back and stay with them.

But Lisa wasn't there. She was on a soccer field running up
to the girl who had control of the ball. Just as she got close enough
to make a play, the girl gave it the hardest kick she could. The ball
hit Lisa in the stomach, and knocked the air out of her. All the other
girls sat down in place as the coaches and the referee ran up to her.
A moment later, she stood up and walked to the side of the field,
replaced in the game by a teammate. Her mother walked around
the field to sit with her on the blanket the team was using instead
of a bench. Lisa laid her head in her mom's lap. She wanted to go
home. She was tired and crabby and her tummy hurt.

"Lisa, you can't leave, the game isn't over. You're part of a
team, and even if you don't go back out and play, your team still
needs you. You can't just leave because you aren't having fun.

Let's finish out this game and see how you feel." Her mom kissed her forehead and headed back to the parents' side of the field.

Before the game was over, Lisa approached the coach and asked to go back in. She didn't score a goal, but she finished the game. As the family walked to the car Lisa's mom leaned over and whispered, "I'm proud of you."

The man who pulled her out of the water was now taking over CPR. Before he put his lips over hers to start breathing he moved to her ears and said "Come back to us. Somebody down here still needs you."

Suddenly Lisa coughed up water, gasping for air. When she finally stopped, she looked around and found herself surrounded by strange men. Then the memories of the last thirteen hours came rushing back. The man pulled her into his chest and held her as she sobbed. He didn't try to stop her, he just rocked back and forth.

"My name is Robert. Who are you?"

"I'm Lisa."

"Welcome back, Lisa."

Barbara Nell Perrin

Barbara Nell Perrin was born in Bremerton, Washington, but grew up and lived for many years in Brooklyn, New York, before relocating to Central Ohio. She currently lives in Westerville with two dogs, and her son Martin when he returns for vacations from college in Hawaii.

Barbara has worked for various book publishers in sales, marketing and publicity positions, and also served for several years as Editor of *Research Alert*, a newsletter covering research on consumer behavior. She currently is Managing Editor of the *Journal of Alternative and Complementary Medicine* and of *Medical Acupuncture*.

When not busy editing, Barbara writes fiction and poetry. She is a winner of the Women Who Write Annual Poetry and Short Prose Contest and has two Editor's Choice awards from Fiction Writers Platform (www.fictionwritersplatform.net).

Her story about Kevin Bannister was inspired by her own father's struggle with dementia and his recent move to a nursing home.

ESCAPE FROM PALISADES MANOR

By Barbara Nell Perrin

Kevin managed to maneuver himself around the guardrail and creep down onto the floor from his low bed, then crawl toward the door. He peeked out the door before proceeding, on all fours, toward the end of the hall. Passing the first door on his right, he counted "one" under his breath, passing the second "two." There were four doors in all to the bend in the hall that led to the door marked "EXIT." He had barely passed the third door when a large pair of clogs, sprouting a thick pair of legs, appeared suddenly before him.

"Mr. Bannister! What are you doing out of bed?" barked Nurse Caruthers, peering down at him over a beefy pair of crossed arms. "Code blue!" she called, then "Orderly!" and the two of them frog-marched Kevin back to his room. "You're not allowed to leave yet," Caruthers scolded Kevin. Her words were accompanied by rhythmic pressure on his chest and then a tube thrust down his throat.

Kevin remembered arriving at Palisades Manor to visit his Aunty Irma some days ago. He had tried, unsuccessfully, to keep count of how many days. Aunty Irma had been in Palisades' Alzheimer's unit for some years—he forgot how many—and he always came to visit on Sundays. He'd always thought that "manor" was a silly name for the place, as it was just a sprawling building tucked behind a few trees just outside the center of town, with no grounds whatsoever. Pretentious is what it was, and Kevin hated anything pretentious. Somehow, on his last visit, he recalled, he had been mistaken for a patient and not allowed to leave.

He was grateful that Nurse Caruthers called him Mr. Bannister. Everyone else there seemed to call him Kevin, or even Kev, which was a damned impolite way to behave toward someone you didn't even know. No one but Kevin called Nurse Caruthers by her name, they all just called her "Nurse." At least in his mind, for he seemed to have lost his ability to speak. He would open his mouth, yet nothing but a croak, followed by a sigh, would come out.

This had not been Kevin's first attempt to escape. He forgot how many other times there had been—maybe three. The first time, it seemed to him, he had not made it even to the first door on his right. The second time, he did. The first door seemed to lead to a family at Sunday dinner and reminded Kevin of life with Aunty Irma when he was a boy. A cocker spaniel sat at attention under the table, one paw on his young master's knee, hoping for a few bites of the meal. Kevin usually complied, to the surreptitious amusement of the adults gathered there.

He'd always detested vegetables, except for spinach, probably due to Popeye's influence. Aunty Irma knew this and always had a dish of spinach for him, no matter what the rest of the family ate—peas, broccoli, green beans. On Sundays there was usually company, and cinnamon buns for dessert. And after the cinnamon buns were demolished, he and his dog PeeWee could meet up with his buddy Jack Davis and go fishing in Alum Creek, or swimming in warm weather.

The third time he tried to escape, he made it to the second door. Through the second door was what looked like a jungle, with something like tiki lights. Kevin shivered as he remembered his time in Burma during the Second World War, with bullets whizzing over his head as he and Don Allen, his foxhole mate, hunkered down. Funny how he could remember Don all these years later, but he couldn't remember someone he met just yesterday.

Kevin had been a radio operator during the war, tapping out messages in Morse code. But his unit was behind enemy lines and any radio transmissions would likely be picked up by the Japanese. So he was sent through the jungle on foot to deliver a message to another American unit. "Better you than me," laughed Don as Kevin set out. "See ya!"

As Kevin slogged through the jungle, an American G.I. suddenly emerged from the undergrowth and told Kevin, "Go another hundred yards in that direction and you'll be in the middle of a Jap camp. You want to go that way," he said, pointing to Kevin's left, and merged back into the jungle as quickly as he'd appeared. Kevin wondered if this had been a hallucination. But he followed the man's advice and arrived safely at the other American camp. Kevin learned when he got back to his own unit that Don had been killed when a grenade hit their foxhole.

The third door would make this Kevin's fourth attempt at escape. Two more and he might make it through the final door, the one that beckoned. He spent a lot of time thinking about numbers and patterns and trying to make sense of the world around him— the Palisades Manor world—through these numbers and patterns. But just as Kevin thought the patterns were beginning to make sense, they would break apart, like the picture on a television during a storm.

Kevin waited until very late one night for his next attempt— nearly morning, really—reasoning that the staff would be tired and perhaps if not actually asleep at least preoccupied with watching the televisions that seemed to go all night somewhere in the building. And perhaps Nurse Caruthers, who seemed always to be the one who caught him, might be off duty. She couldn't possibly work all the time. He imagined himself creeping down past the guardrail on his bed, onto all fours, and began very quietly, very carefully, to creep along the hall, past door one, door two, door three.

Door three opened onto a college campus, much like OSU, where Kevin had attended on the G.I. Bill. He'd spent some of the happiest times of his life there. He'd met Genevieve Rein, the love of his life. But when Kevin opened a bookstore rather than going on to graduate studies, Genevieve's parents had been horrified. Everyone in their family, they argued, was "well educated," by which they meant that the underachievers possessed mere master's degrees. They launched an all-out attack on "that crazy beatnik," persuading Gen that she needed to abandon Kevin.

Kevin was just abreast of door four, the entrance to a bookstore with a "going out of business" sign on it, and next to it, a large poster thanking his customers for forty years of business. It had been a good forty years. There were easy chairs and couches in Kevin's store, and a coffee pot that was always on, long before most booksellers thought of offering these things. The front door of Bannister's Books was rarely locked, much to the amusement—and sometimes the dismay—of his neighbors. More than a few travelers found a place to sleep at Bannister's over the years, usually repaying Kevin with some work in the store.

There was always a dog in the store, sometimes two. Kevin

77

adopted older dogs that the local shelter had trouble placing because of their age. He remembered the books, and the dogs, and thought, now it's gone, all gone. Through his tears, the clogs sprouting thick legs suddenly loomed before him.

"If I didn't know better, I might think you wanted to leave us, Mr. Bannister," barked Nurse Caruthers, towering above him. She called an orderly, and just like that, he was back in his railed bed.

"Now how could you possibly think that?" Kevin thought sarcastically. He would have liked to say it if he could. He suspected that they had started to give him sedatives to keep him from trying to escape. He always seemed so tired these days, and so slow and lethargic. His habit of creeping about on all fours during these escape attempts was only partly to remain obscure. He wasn't sure if he could stand if he tried. And he was too tired to try, and too scared that he would find he could not stand if he did.

On his sixth try, Kevin made it right up almost to the door that says "EXIT." But Nurse Caruthers was always there, always ready to prevent his reaching its comfort. If the pattern holds true, thought Kevin as he was frog-marched back to his room, chest-pressed and intubated, I may be able to make it through to the light next time.

By now Kevin had become quite adept at crawling toward the door that would lead him to clarity, and with each attempt his progress had seemed faster. So when, a night or two nights or maybe three later—he couldn't remember which—when he made his seventh attempt, he was actually able to reach up, grasp the door handle, open the door, and hurl himself through. Funny thing though, what was on the other side of the door was just his room, with the low bed with the railing, the TV he never watched, and the closet that presumably held the clothes he'd been wearing when he arrived. And Nurse Caruthers gazing down on him, arms folded, barking, "Mr. Bannister!"

Kevin was confused. He was confused much of the time these days. But now he was more confused than ever. Why would a door that says "EXIT" lead back to his room, which was on the other side of the hall and at least a hundred feet away? Something about the place just didn't make sense.

Doc Wadsworth was there too, in Kevin's room, conferring

with Nurse Caruthers. They called him in after each of Kevin's escape attempts, and he usually gave Kevin a shot of something that made him feel very tired and unable to move.

"This was the worst one yet," Kevin heard Nurse Caruthers say softly to Doc Wadsworth. But his eyelids grew heavy and he drifted away before he could hear the doctor's reply.

Kevin imagined that the shots of whatever it was were becoming stronger each time—at least they seemed to him to work faster and faster. When he wasn't trying to escape, they just gave him drugs by mouth. But Kevin hated pills and tried to spit them out, or waited until the attendant left and then spit them out. But he must have been discovered, probably when the wet pills were found stuck to the floor of his room. Instead, they fed him applesauce and he suspected that they had crushed the pills and mixed them in. But he loved applesauce—always had, ever since he was a kid—and did not have the fortitude to resist its lure.

Thus sedated, it was a while before Kevin was able to make another attempt at the enticing door to freedom. Time was still a blur in Kevin's mind, and it was difficult for him to judge exactly how long, but he thought maybe two or three days at least.

"We almost lost you that time, Mr. Bannister," Nurse Caruthers barked down at him as he lay in his bed. This time it was a gentle bark, almost more of a woof, and although her face displayed annoyance, it was mixed with concern. It reminded him of the way Aunty Irma looked down at him when he'd been sick with scarlet fever.

Kevin often thought about his Aunty Irma, who had practically raised him—Aunty Irma and Uncle George. Aunty Irma was one of the few people he could remember clearly. One of the last times he'd seen her, she'd glared at him—Aunty Irma almost never glared—and insisted "Irma and George should be together!" as though someone were trying deliberately to keep George and Irma apart. She'd been in her eighties at the time and had lost George to a stroke more than twenty years earlier. It was the only thing she'd said in years that made any sense at all, and a few months later she was dead.

The funeral had been well-attended and many people had tried to comfort Kevin by saying that it was for the best—after all, she'd lived a long life and a good one, and had earned her rest. These days, Kevin thought more and more about Aunty Irma, and could almost picture her holding her arms out and calling to him.

He visualized the door that said "EXIT" and the release it represented as he lay on his bed. And just beyond the door he saw a smiling Aunty Irma, her arms held out to him. He had to make it through that door to be with Aunty Irma and Uncle George, to be free of the pain, and of the brief snatches of embarrassment, to be young and healthy and loved again.

Having once made it through that door before something went wrong, Kevin was sure that he could do so again. Past the guardrail, onto the floor, through the door, past doors one, two, three and four, approaching the final door, and there was Aunty Irma, with Uncle George just behind her. Through the door, and it all vanished.

Kevin was back in his room with Nurse Caruthers looking down on him, shaking her head and woofing "Mr. Bannister!" And Doc Wadsworth preparing an injection. And Kevin seemed to be attached to the machines again, their tubes running into and out of him. It was damned uncomfortable, and he couldn't imagine what would make one person want to do something like that to another person. And he felt so very, very tired that he couldn't even think about making it through the door another time.

Kevin felt himself drifting on clouds and no longer even noticed whether Nurse Caruthers or another of the staff were around him. When he had the strength to think, he thought of Aunty Irma and Uncle George, of his mom and dad, whom he could barely remember, of his childhood friend Jack with whom he'd fished in Alum Creek, of his Army buddy Don, and of Genevieve. He thought of the bookstore he'd run for forty years until the big chains put him out of business. He wondered if there'd be books in Heaven. There must be—it is Heaven, after all.

It was some time before Kevin managed to gather the strength necessary for another assault on the door that said "EXIT." Past the guardrail, onto the floor, through the door, past doors one, two, three and four and, approaching the final door, there was Aunty Irma.

"Aunty Irma," Kevin exclaimed, "I've been looking all over

for you!" Aunty Irma was young and pretty again, and Uncle George was just behind her. Through the door, and he was suddenly young again, and laughing, in Aunty Irma's arms.

Back in his room, surrounded by tubes and machines, Nurse Caruthers pressed her lips together and tried to keep from crying. Mr. Bannister had been one of her favorites. "He wasn't always like this," she told Doc Wadsworth in a quavering voice. "When I was a girl, I loved the Cherry Ames books; they're what made me want to become a nurse." A gentle chuckle at the thought interrupted her. "We never had any money for books in my house. But Mr. Bannister had a whole shelf of second-hand Cherry Ames in his store, and every week he would find a job for me to do—feed his dogs, dust some shelves—so that I could take one home. He even moved them into the back room so no one else could buy them.

"I needed tuition money when I was in nursing school, and he gave me a job," she continued through sniffles. "Mostly I just sat there and studied, and made good money doing it. And I wasn't the only one."

Doc Wadsworth gently laid a hand on her arm, "We did everything we could, it was just his time to go."

Nurse Caruthers sighed and went on to her next patient.

Cynthia Rosi

After graduating from college, Cynthia Rosi immigrated from Seattle to London, England, determined to write for a living. She worked in journalism to pay the bills, and wrote poetry and fiction on the side. At the turn of the millennium, Headline, UK published Cynthia's two mystery novels *Motherhunt* and *Butterfly Eyes* (now on e-book).

In 2003, Cynthia moved with her husband to Columbus, Ohio. She spent time raising a family, and helping her husband start Via Vecchia Winery, before picking up her writing career once again. You can see her writing in *The Short North Gazette*, as well as in a variety of wine magazines.

Cynthia consults with businesses on their social media presence, in addition to freelance gigs. She also runs the Columbus Writer's Network, which assists writers looking for professional opportunities.

To reach Cynthia about this story or her services as a freelance writer, she can be contacted via her website, www.cynthiarosi.com, or at cynthiarosi@gmail.com.

"Smoke in My Hands" is a piece of creative non-fiction; the events took place as they've been described

SMOKE IN MY HANDS

By Cynthia Rosi

When I recall my father, I recall him towering above me, and his huge hand which fit over my own small one like a baseball mitt over a hardball. A baseball mitt smelled like my father—woodsy and slightly sweaty, with machine oil, in the way of carpenters, or carvers. I was nose-high to his leather tool belt, his flannel shirt-tail smeared with sawdust.

I remember walking with him to the A&P on a day filled with sunshine and being swept up and carried on his shoulders when I complained about my tired legs. I felt so comfortable with my hands wrapped under Dad's chin, my wrists pressed against his black, horned-rim glasses, looking down at the top of his bald head. I could wrap my feet under his armpits and balance myself while he crossed his arms over his chest and kept striding.

On the way back from the grocery store, I would have to walk, because Dad carried the groceries in paper sacks on his shoulders: bacon, ice cream, eggs, cheese, flour, butter, and whole milk. I would hold onto a belt loop, or walk by his side, and we would stop several times in the three blocks home, resting as we stood on the sidewalk, gazing past the houses out to Puget Sound, to the glimmer of sun on water, like diamonds scattered over a wood-saw blade.

As the apples fell from our backyard tree, and we stewed them for sauce, Dad would haul logs home from Alki Beach in his broad-fendered Ford truck. He chain-sawed the logs into lengths, and with an ax split them into quarters and eighths against a wide old stump, chucking the firewood through our coal chute down into the cellar.

Come October, Dad built a fire in the fireplace, and my brothers and sister and I would sprawl with him in front of it, absorbing the heat, watching the magic of orange flames transmuting wood from solid logs into a silvery heap of ash. I felt like I knew how those orange coals tasted, that I could pick up a coal and put it into my mouth. Mesmerized by the fire, I would put my ear against Dad's chest, listening to sound reverberate as he spoke, then lift my ear to hear the burr of his normal voice, and put my head against his chest again, his voice strange like whale song, or talking under water.

I would listen to his heart beat and it frightened me, because my brothers told me you couldn't live without your heart beating. Dad's heartbeat seemed terribly slow. My heartbeats trotted along, three beats to his one. His seemed sonorous, but hesitant, an unsteady drum.

Looking back, I can't sort the jumble of that time into a proper order. It's like a toy-box, stuffed with dolls and teddy bears: the horse phase, the Barbies phase, the doll that pees, Raggedy Ann and Andy, and crumpled at the bottom an old yellow blankie, with sateen edges, my first pun. "This is my dragon blanket," I'd told my mother. "Because I'm always draggin' it around."

Like the toy-box, I remember a jumble of who he was. Chauffeur: driving us to church on Easter Sunday, my sister and I in black patent leather shoes, wearing white gloves and Easter dresses, carefully carrying purses, in which we'd each keep our quarter for the collection. Builder: painting and sawing, hammering at jobs around the house. Friend: defending us against Mom, her disciplines, her regimens and routines. Companion: listening to our prayers at night, sitting us on his knee at dinner, walking in front of us on family hikes.

Driving on I-5 from Seattle to Tacoma, we saw a billboard with two black-lettered lines: "Will the last person leaving Seattle please turn out the lights?" Boeing had laid off its engineers, including Dad. As the unemployment benefits evaporated, our formal dining room morphed into a dance studio. Mom taught the neighborhood kids to *arabesque* and *pirouette*, to *plié* and *relevé* at a wooden barre sanded by Dad. This wasn't the deal Mom had signed up for, the woman paying the bills with checks brought in by her tiny pupils, feeding her family by tapping her feet, fingers clicking off the beats as little girls in pink tights, pink leotards, and pink tutus learned to sashay in a line and twirl in unison.

This wasn't the deal Dad had signed up for when he earned his degree in Engineering at the University of Washington, when he joined the Air Force at the end of World War II, when he landed that position at a rock-solid company like Boeing. The recession bit, jobs disappeared, and this was the deal they got.

As the apple tree's leaves turned from green to gold, and to plum, then fell to the ground, as summer showers turned into thunderstorms, our home became tense. One November night, my brothers fought with my sister. Dad chased the boys around with a broom even though he was feeling sick, herding us all up to bed; no kisses, and no prayers.

In my dreams, I found myself in a tunnel, like a huge, concrete outflow pipe, its walls the color of cement. As I looked up the tunnel, I saw the end of it was the color of oyster shells, like sunlight behind clouds.

I knew Dad was at the end of this tunnel. I could feel his presence behind the color of white, as if he stood behind a giant door made of white clouds. I began to walk up the tunnel, to follow him. I walked until I seemed to be half way to the end of that big, concrete pipe.

A voice spoke inside of me and said: "Your father is dead. But you will see him again after a long, long time."

In my mind I heard a number: 76. I argued with this voice. "No he's not! Mom and Dad have been fighting. They're going to get a divorce." But as I said it, I knew this was what I wished would happen. I tried to keep walking up the tunnel, to reach my Dad. Instead, I found myself back on my horsehair mattress, my pillow pressed against the maple headboard, awake, an unwelcome resurrection. I would rather have stayed with my Dad.

I glanced over at my bedside clock and saw the time: 7:30 a.m. I'd overslept. Mom would be mad, and I would be late walking to school.

Mom cracked open my door, and I saw a slice of her face, her red nose, and bloodshot eyes. She said, "Cynthia, you don't have to go to school today."

I said, "I know, Dad's dead."

She didn't hear me. "I have sad news. Daddy died last night."

He had gone up the pipe and disappeared behind the door, and stayed in the place where I wasn't allowed until the number 76.

What would have happened if the voice had let me through? Would I be dead now, too?

I sat next to a cold fireplace, watching a small flame lick the blackened remainder of a log. I whittled a stick with my pocket knife, the way Dad whittled sticks, the way I'd seen him teach my brothers. My brother Douglas looked like a shell, a lifeless doll propped against the sofa. My brother Stephen cried in a way I'd never seen him cry before; not from rage or frustration, but from an abyss of grief.

That afternoon my mother sent us kids to the movies, our cousin Julie driving a VW Bus to "A Night at the Opera" with Groucho Marx, at the Admiral Theater where Dad had taken us, a bag of his own butter-popped corn slipped under his raincoat.

I laughed my guts out at Groucho, waggling his cigar, his silly walk, and at Harpo, my favorite, tooting his horn. I laughed until my belly cramped, like someone being tickled to the point of torture, and when I could draw breath, I thought: *I will live my life without seeing him again.* What would it be like to be nine, or turn ten, and not see him? To graduate from high school? To get married, and not have him there? I couldn't imagine that it was over. A part of my life had finished, to be set in amber, those lively memories preserved, shrunken into photos, into old clothes that smelled like he smelled.

I kept his construction helmet under my bed, day-glo orange, and would pull it out and stick my face in it and inhale, until someone cleaned out under my bed, and stole the helmet from me. I kept a sweaty shirt he'd go running in, a green wool shirt from the Air Force, and wore it into holes until I was twenty-five. I swiped his dog tags, and his Sigma Chi pin and took them to college. The possessions of a father are so tiny, compared to the rich memories of a small child.

In the place of a father, I had a dream to sustain me, as ephemeral as smoke in my hands.

Bradley Nelson

Bradley Nelson grew up in a small town in the southeastern corner of Washington (the state, not the university, nor the nation's capital). In elementary school he wrote poetry for his own amusement. In college he was granted an adaptation license to write and stage a novel by C.S. Lewis, and had poetry published in a campus anthology. Following graduation he worked for two years in the media relations office for his alma mater, writing articles for various campus publications, including a cover article for the college's alumni magazine.

Later, when Bradley decided to set off and explore the world, he got side-tracked in Ohio. The place has grown on him over the past eight years, but he still can't quite understand the fuss locals make over the Buckeyes.

Bradley lives with his partner Kurt and his cat Shadow. Both are forgiving of his writing habits, which are random at best. Bradley is currently working on an adaptation of his favorite Shakespearean play: A Midsummer Night's Dream.

Bradley would like to thank Columbus Creative Cooperative for providing the inspiration and motivation to write "The Strange Case of John Doe." This is his first published short story.

THE STRANGE CASE OF JOHN DOE

By Bradley Nelson

The world ended suddenly, in the darkest purple imaginable. When he came to, he was disoriented. Upon opening his eyes, he felt like he was falling, slowly.

"Can you hear me, sir?"

His vision was blurry, but he could vaguely make out the shape of the speaker. Someone was leaning over him, lit in flashing red and white.

"Are you hurt?"

He tried to make sense of the question. *Was* he hurt? Instinctively, he reached for his face. Or tried to. His brain sent the signals, but his arms were unresponsive. He felt unplugged—disconnected. With great concentration, he sent another mental order to lift his arm, but he was only partially successful. His arms seemed to be strapped at his sides. When he tried to move his head to get a better view of where he was, he discovered his neck was also held securely in place.

"Please don't try to move. We don't know the extent of your injuries."

For a brief moment his vision began to darken. The sensation of falling was worse when he closed his eyes.

"Stay with me, sir! Keep your eyes open, if you can."

He opened his eyes, and blinked repeatedly, trying to clear his vision.

"That's better. How do you feel?"

"What . . . " he started to say, but speaking was even more difficult than moving had been.

The voice continued, "We believe you've been in some sort of accident. Are you in any pain?"

He thought for a moment. No, there wasn't any pain. Should there be? Was that bad? He tried to shake his head, then managed to form a single word, "No."

A face filled his vision, then a bright light was shined first in one eye, then the other.

"Welcome back to the world of the living. You were unresponsive earlier. Do you remember what happened?"

He struggled to recall. "No."

"Someone reported seeing you lying on the side of the road. We're not sure how long you were there, but you were unconscious. Also you were naked. Do you have any idea where your clothes might be?"

"No?"

He hadn't noticed being naked before. Now he realized he was covered with a thin sheet. He shivered.

"Can you tell me your name?"

He thought for a moment. "I can't remember." He didn't know his name. What had happened?

"What year is it?"

He concentrated. These should be easy questions, but his brain was full of fog. "I don't know."

"Okay, Mister John Doe. Do you mind if I call you John? My name is Franklin. My partner Jesse and I are going to load you into the ambulance now. Okay? Let us know if it causes you any pain. One . . . Two . . . "

There was a sudden movement, and then his vision was filled with the brightly lit interior of the ambulance. He could see wires, equipment, small boxes. Everything looked vaguely familiar, but he couldn't place anything, couldn't put names to them. The sensation of falling also returned. Stronger this time than before.

"Falling . . . " he said aloud.

"We've got you secured, sir."

He felt a hand touching his wrist, and something cold on his chest. He closed his eyes. Let the experts deal with the situation. He couldn't remember anything, good or bad, about his life. He couldn't even remember his name. He couldn't think of a single thing to keep him grounded.

"I'm losing the pulse! Sir? Hang on, keep your eyes open!"

He opened his eyes again, slowly, but it was a tremendous effort. Everything was a brightly-lit blur. Purple tendrils crept in from the edges of his vision.

"I think he may be crashing!"

He couldn't tell if his eyes were still open or not.

"Ready, defib!"

All he could see were a hundred different shades of purple, and he continued to fall.

"Charging . . . "

The darkness pulled at him, forcefully, like a strong magnetic attraction. The darkness called to him. It even spoke his name: *Mikviel . . .* Mikviel? Yes, that felt right. The darkness knew his name. Perhaps it was time to let go.

Mikviel . . .

"Clear!"

Everything came back into sharp focus. He could see a light fixture in the center of his vision. He could see two people, one on either side of him. One was holding something in either hand.

". . . heartbeat appears to be stabilizing."

With a jolt, Mikviel was flooded with fragmented memories: a room filled with virtual display monitors . . . towering electro-coils . . . a human-sized Transfer Capsule . . .

"—no, wait, we're losing him again. Charge!"

Some part of his brain told him to fight, to stay awake no

matter what, but another part told him that he was falling, that falling was inevitable, and that he shouldn't struggle so much.

"Clear!"

Mikviel remembered himself.

He had been selected because he had no family to miss him if the Transfer was unsuccessful. He reminded himself that previous attempts on animals had been successful (the most recent ones, at least).

"Mikviel, are you sure you want to do this?"

This was his chance to back out. He wanted to say no, but he knew this was an important moment for science. "I'm sure."

"Ready?"

"Ready."

"All clear. Initiate Transfer protocol sequence: T-H-Zero-Zero-One"

The hatch on the Transfer Capsule closed and sealed automatically. He could hear the hum of the power coils charging, but the sound was muted. As the capsule began to fill with purple fluid, he tensed, then forced himself to relax. No turning back now.

Then he was here, with these two men. Looking into the faces above him, he tried to speak, but again his body failed him so he focused on memorizing the two figures working intently to save his life. The one who had tried to talk to him earlier was light-skinned, brown haired, with facial hair trimmed to cover only the mouth and chin area. The second was darker-skinned, round face, black hair, no facial hair.

He searched for something more conclusive. He needed something to identify Time and Place. Both men wore similar clothes, a uniform presumably—solid, dark blue in color, open collar, pockets on both sides, and a white emblem with the image of a flame in the center. Above the flame: *Columbus Ohio*. Below:

Division of Fire. He committed the logo and its text to memory.

The darkness returned so suddenly and with such force, that he didn't have time to resist.

The two paramedics filed a strange report that night. It began with a description of resuscitating an unconscious man found by the side of the road, and it ended in a confused account of the man disappearing before their very eyes. Their supervisor dismissed it as a prank, and the two men were reprimanded for improper use of equipment. The incident was, more or less, quickly forgotten.

Wayne Rapp

Wayne Rapp has been a professional writer and film/video producer since leaving the University of Arizona with a degree in English. After a career in corporate communications in California, Michigan, and Ohio, he decided to work for himself. Through his company, It's A Rapp Productions, located in Columbus, he produces films and videos for corporations and advertising/ marketing agencies. As a freelance writer, he also writes business-related articles for trade journals and other print media. His work has taken him to most of the fifty states and to thirteen foreign countries.

He has written two books, *Celebrating, Honoring, and Valuing Rich Traditions: The History of the Ohio Appalachian Arts Program* for the Ohio Arts Council and *Drawn to the Living Water: Twenty Years of Spiritual Discovery* for The Spirituality Network.

Wayne has also written numerous short stories, essays, and nonfiction pieces for publication. A collection of short stories, *Burnt Sienna*, was a finalist for the Miguel Mármol Award. His short story, "In the Time of Marvel and Confusion," was nominated for a Pushcart Prize. His creative writing has twice been honored with Individual Artist Excellence Awards from the Ohio Arts Council. He has lectured on writing at The Ohio State University and Ohio Wesleyan University and taught in the Thurber House Summer Writing Camp.

Fort Walton Beach, in the Florida panhandle, was a favorite Easter vacation destination for Wayne and his family when his children were younger.

RETURN TO FORT WALTON BEACH
By Wayne Rapp

Jane listened to her son Brad talking and thought how like his father he was: tall, dark hair already beginning to thin in front, too early for his thirty-five years. His body was beginning to show age, but his face was friendly and kind, and like his father, he could be very persuasive when he pressed a point. And that's what he was doing at the moment.

"Mom, it's all planned. The date has been on everybody's calendar for a year."

"Oh, I'm not trying to ruin anyone's vacation. You all go and have a good time. It's just still too early for me."

Brad persisted, "But that's just why you should go. You don't want to stay here alone. Fort Walton Beach has always been a family thing, ever since we were kids. I think Marianne was in middle school the first time we went down there."

"Fourth grade," Marianne corrected her brother. "And Janice was twelve, and you were fifteen."

"That means we've been going for twenty years, Mom. That's a milestone; that's an anniversary. We've got to celebrate that for sure."

"So go and celebrate," she urged.

"An anniversary for all of us, Mom. You can't quit on us now. You've been spending too much time alone. We need you with us. It's not Easter vacation without you."

This was just the way Phil used to push the girls when they were younger, she thought. Now his son was doing the same thing, and she was one of the girls that needed pushing.

"Brad . . . Brad, I don't think I can yet."

"You can, for sure. You'll ride down with Marcia and me and the kids. We've got plenty of room for five people. Marianne and Janice are going to try to cram their families into one van. It'll be tight, but they'll have fun together going down. We can take some of their stuff if they're too jammed together. We'll caravan down, stay overnight at that place in Alabama that we all like, and get into

Fort Walton Beach by mid-afternoon." Brad was describing the same route that she and her husband, Phil, had charted twenty years earlier, making it sound like he'd just laid it out.

"Brad, I'll give it some thought; that's all I can promise."

But after both Marianne and Janice called pleading with her to come, and Brad returned to plead in person, she sighed and relented. "I'll come and help watch the kids, so you parents can get some time to yourselves."

"Mom, we don't need you for a babysitter. We want you to enjoy yourself, too. You don't need to do anything. Of course, if you want to make chicken parmesan or lasagna for dinner one night, you are more than welcome." He smiled and pulled her into an embrace. "Dad'll be with us," he said. "He wouldn't miss our twentieth anniversary."

Oh, but he would. By six months. It was April, and his heart had stopped unexpectedly the previous November. He'd missed Thanksgiving, Christmas, New Years, and his sixtieth birthday. Now he would miss Easter, and the family's twentieth trek from Ohio to Fort Walton Beach, Florida, and she didn't know how she could possibly make it through the week without him.

Jane stood in front of her full-length mirror holding a bathing suit in front of her, and taking inventory of her fifty-nine-year-old body, with sagging breasts and hips that had spread from carrying and birthing three children. What she probably hated most were the dimpled tops of her legs, with blue veins showing through. She was holding a three-year-old bathing suit, but she knew that no suit was going to cover up that much damage. Jane shrugged and added the suit to the stack of clothing to pack for the trip. She made up her mind that she would wear it and not care what others might think.

Phil had always urged her to adopt that attitude. "You are such a beautiful person inside and out," he'd said to her. "Who could possibly look past all that goodness to search for body faults?" Eventually she had almost started believing it herself. She flipped her silver-streaked hair, smiled tentatively at her reflection in the mirror, and started packing.

Nearly every town they came to on the trip to Fort Walton

Beach conjured a memory. Traveling the same route for twenty years meant they'd stopped in most of them at one time or another, if only to fill up with fuel or buy ice cream cones. Here was the town where they'd had to stay overnight when they'd blown a tire and the spare was flat, waiting until morning before the local Sears was open and they could claim a replacement tire on their warranty. They hadn't arrived at Fort Walton until late at night that year. And here was the town where they'd had to get Marianne to the emergency room when she'd been stung by a bee during a lunch break and her face had swollen to a grotesque mask. They'd been so shaken and thankful she'd survived, they'd considered turning around and going home. But Marianne wouldn't let them, so they had forged ahead, and it had been one of their best vacations ever, even though the weather was frigid that year.

It was even colder when the three families and Jane arrived at Fort Walton Beach this year. The weather was always iffy around Easter, whether the holiday fell in March or April. Fort Walton Beach was in the Florida Panhandle and did not enjoy the much warmer weather of Central and South Florida. But when it was warm, the sugar-white soft sand put the area in a class of its own.

Jane was walking barefoot on the sand, even though the lack of sunshine put a dull cast on its surface. The grandchildren had all been dropped off at the aquarium. Their parents had stayed behind, the men playing cards in one of the suites while the women were grocery shopping, buying what provisions they'd need for a couple of days.

Jane was glad she'd brought a sweater. She pulled it closer around her and rubbed her arms as she began to shiver. She continued trudging through the sand, inching toward the water, stepping in bravely for a few seconds. The icy water made her toes tingle and she felt more alert than she had in a long time. She thought of the many times she and Phil had walked together late at night, holding on to each other and letting the ocean breezes tickle their bodies and heighten their desire.

They were always like new lovers in Fort Walton Beach. When they'd first started coming for Easter vacation and were

97

trying to make sure the money would last the week, they'd all stayed in one room with two doubles and a roll-away. After a few years, when Phil was making more money, they'd found a place that rented suites. There was a master bedroom, two baths, a kitchen and a living room with a couch that converted to a queen-size bed and a smaller couch that could be used as a single. The girls slept together in the queen and Brad, regardless of how much he grew, was always happy in the single. That left Jane and Phil to enjoy the private bedroom. And enjoy they did.

She wrapped her arms around herself while she walked and remembered. They always tried to reserve rooms that were gulf-side and at least three stories up, so they could see over the dunes to the water. One night they were on the fifth floor, and after a satisfying period of love making, she fell into a blissful slumber, still locked in his arms. She wasn't sure how much time had passed, but she was in the shadow of wakefulness when she heard the patio door slide open. She sat up in bed to see her husband standing outside on the patio. He was completely naked. He stared into the starry sky, the sound of the gulf's waves crashing below. She got up and searched for her shorts and a T-shirt. He sensed her presence and came closer to the door.

"What are you doing?" he asked.

"Trying to find some clothes so I can join you."

"You don't need anything but yourself," he said. "This is a clothing-optional beach." He took her hand and led her outside. They stood at the rail, alternating their gaze to the starry skies and the glints of light that played off the waves below. Holding hands, they stood in silence for what could have been minutes or hours, sliding quickly backward into the privacy of their bedroom only when they saw a light in the suite next door.

The sun was peeking through the clouds as Jane climbed the stairs to her room. She paused to enjoy the view before opening her door. The beach had begun to take on its classic whiteness, and sunbeams were glinting off the waves under a bright blue sky. This was the Fort Walton Beach that she knew and loved.

The week passed all too quickly. Buoyed by her memories of

long ago days at Fort Walton Beach with her husband and family, Jane relaxed and lived each day as a gift. On the night before they left, she made her famous chicken parmesan. Brad helped her clean up while board games replaced the dishes on the table. He looked at her and smiled. "Are you glad you came?"

"Yes. Thank you for being so insistent." It had been a perfect week, except for one thing. She missed her husband more than ever.

As Jane climbed the stairs from her children's suites to her single room one story up, she could tell the weather was going to change. They had enjoyed sunny, warm weather for a week, but now it was getting colder. She could see clouds gathering to the west and feared they'd be driving at least part of their return trip in rain.

Sometime during the night, the wind rattled the patio door and woke her. She got up with the idea of securing it, but instead, she stood there in the open doorway and listened to the wind. It drew her outside on the balcony where she could see in the flashes of distant lightning the gathering storm clouds closing in. She walked to the rail and looked out. She could not see the dark ocean, but the full force of the waves sounded one crescendo and then another. The wind rippled against her thin nightgown. On impulse, she reached down and pulled it over her head and threw it behind her into the room.

She stood there and let the wind wash over her body, bringing it back to life. She smiled into its full force and shivered at the gentle touch on her shoulder. Phil was with her, she knew. She could feel his caress as his soft hands moved over her body, every part of her tingling in anticipation.

Ramona R. Douglas

Ramona Douglas has always had a love for writing. Originally from Scioto County, Ohio, her family lived in Chicago and Columbus before they grew roots on her stepfather's farm in New Marshfield, Ohio. She calls Athens County "home" because of the lasting friendships and kinships formed in a small town school called Waterloo.

Writing "The Bus Trip," a true-to-life non-fiction account, was an emotionally difficult task. But with the invaluable help from her peers in Columbus Creative Cooperative, she managed to morph the memory of her father into this incredible journey through time.

Ramona writes stories from her own personal experiences. Never short for material, she laughs when she says at her age she has enough to write about until she keels over at the keyboard. Although her stories have a serious undertone, she loves writing humor, irony, and satire.

Ramona and her husband recently moved to the Columbus area from Jackson, Ohio, and have also lived in California and New York. They have two children: a daughter, who is a teacher, and a son, who is a Marine Corps Major. They also have four grandsons.

Ramona is a proud member of Ohio Writers Guild, Grove City Writers Group, and Columbus Creative Cooperative.

THE BUS TRIP
By Ramona R. Douglas

I stood in the doorway, my nose pressed against the screen, and watched my father pick up his clothes, which my mother had thrown into the yard. I turned around and asked, "Can I go out and say goodbye to Daddy?"

She shrieked, "No, you cannot!" He heard her and stopped what he was doing to glance at the door. I smiled at him and started to wave, but he just turned around and walked toward his truck. I watched as he got in, started the engine, and drove down the dirt road, leaving a swirling tunnel of dust behind. I stood there for the longest time, sadly watching the dust settle in the summer heat, waiting to see if he would come back. He didn't.

When my father's letter arrived, it had been nearly ten years since he had driven out of my life, and I was a senior in high school. I stood at the mailbox and stared at the envelope addressed to me. His meticulous handwriting in the upper left corner had a return address in Seattle, Washington. I quickly tore it open, then ran to the house to show my mother. His written request for me to spend the summer with him sent her into a rage that ended with an "Absolutely not!"

In the weeks that followed, I gradually wore my mother down, pleading and begging until she could no longer stand the sound of my voice. My father had said he would fly east to accompany me either by bus or plane—my choice. With much deliberation, I had chosen the bus, opting to fly home. My mother made it plain that although she agreed to let me go, he wasn't welcome on or even *near* our farm. I made arrangements with my aunt and uncle to meet him at their house. I figured even if I didn't know the man, I could at least enjoy the summer away from that miserable farm.

Our small dairy farm was the only income we had. It was stretched way beyond its limits on a good day, and a farm has few good days. My brother had been drafted and was halfway across the world in Vietnam. Every evening, my mother would watch the evening news; listening to reporters give body counts over

101

the deafening gunfire in the background. My sister had recently married and moved out. My stepfather was home from the hospital, but in his recuperative medicated state, he was oblivious to all of this; my mother shouldered it alone. She did have help, however, from the bottles that rattled when the refrigerator door was opened.

On the day I left, my mother cried and made me promise to call her. She said if I ever needed her, she was as close as the phone. She reminded me of my job waiting and not to get any big ideas in my head about not coming back. I carried the guilt trip she gave me along with my suitcase to the car.

I settled into a guest room at my aunt and uncle's, then made small talk as we waited for my father. His flight was due that afternoon, but it was now dark. I could tell by their glances to one another that they didn't expect him to show up. I felt embarrassed for all of us. We were scheduled to leave on the bus the next morning. The longer I waited, the more I resigned myself to the fact that I would have to go back to the farm the next day, and my mother would be saying "I told you so" for the rest of my life.

It was nearly midnight when I heard the clamor out in the kitchen. I knew it was my father, I recognized his voice. I also knew by the sound of his voice that he had been drinking. You don't forget things like that. I frantically looked around the room in a panic, wondering whether to feign sleep or climb out the window and just run away.

I jumped when the door suddenly opened and my aunt whispered "Your dad is here if you want to come out and say hello." I could tell she was upset. Neither she nor my uncle drank, and both had a very little tolerance for those who did. I didn't know what to do, so I reluctantly followed her to the kitchen. She interrupted their loud conversation and announced, "Hey, look who's still awake!"

He was leaning against their kitchen counter with a liquor bottle in his hand. He grinned at me across the room, "Well, helloooo there!" He then looked away and resumed talking to my uncle. I exchanged glances with my aunt. Ten years and this was our reunion? I turned around without saying a word and went back
102

to my room. This can't end well, I thought, not at all.

What little sleep I got that night was interrupted with disturbing dreams of loud cursing, pleading cries, the sounds of slaps and punches, and the noise of glass breaking. A bedroom window was quietly raised and three small children climbed out into the cold night air under the cover of darkness, listening to their mother's urgent whispers . . . "Run, run toward the woods, don't look back, just run!"

The next morning we didn't say a word to each other. He ate his breakfast and made small talk with my uncle. My aunt was fussing over me, giving me a few dollars "for mad money, just in case" with a wink. I had no clue what that meant but mumbled a thank you and stuffed it down in my purse.

At the bus station, my aunt handed me a shopping bag from Martings Department Store. "I thought you'd like to wear this on your way out." She had a big smile on her face. I pulled out a long, flowing dress with a bright floral print. It wasn't what I would have chosen, but I took the bag and thanked her.

She rubbed my shoulder and said, "You can change in the restroom." In the ladies room I put on the new outfit and shoved my old, worn-out clothes in my suitcase.

When my father and I boarded our bus, he pointed to our seats and told me to sit near the window. I saw my aunt and uncle standing outside. My aunt pointed in our direction, waving and smiling. Waving back, I returned her smile. She had no idea how nervous and scared I was. I suddenly missed my mother and that pitiful farm.

My father and I pretty much ignored each other from Portsmouth to Cincinnati. I stared out the window at the scenery along the Ohio River and he stared ahead watching the road in front of us. Out of the corner of my eye, I saw him take a small flat bottle out of his jacket pocket and turn his head away from me to take a swig. I looked back out the window. He was more of a stranger to me than a father. A drunken stranger. I remembered him writing that he had quit drinking. His word was beginning to hold the same weight with me that it did with my mother. What was I doing getting on a bus and traveling across the country with him? I started plotting ways to escape.

As we stepped off the bus in Cincinnati, my father looked around and said "Now stick real close and hold onto me, because you could get lost in here." I did as he said, taking hold of his jacket. It crossed my mind this would be the perfect place to escape but I continued to clutch the back of his jacket. The smell of diesel and the city stench from the afternoon heat permeated the air, stinging my nose as we entered the bus station doors.

Everyone was in a hurry and several travelers bumped into us as we walked through the crowd. He checked the connecting departure and I followed him across the terminal to board our next bus. I nervously looked around and tightened my grip on his jacket as he carried our suitcases. A fleeting thought went through my head; he'd probably want a drink as soon as we boarded our next bus. I thought about asking him if I could have a swig from the flat bottle, too.

The tires made a loud hum on the pavement. I couldn't see anything out the window after dark, so I would sneak glances at my father. He had aged; his now-thin hair was close-cropped and grey. He wore a neatly pressed shirt under a denim jacket, jeans, and plain black cowboy boots. His face had a worn, tired look. His gnarled knuckles were prominent as he held a paper cup in his hands. He took swigs from the hidden bottle every so often, then would spit the juice of his chewing tobacco into the cup. I glanced around at the other passengers, a little embarrassed by this. Mail Pouch, I remembered. Through the years, every time I saw a barn with Mail Pouch painted on the side, it had made me think of him. I remembered when he had given me a small pinch when I was little. I had tasted it and quickly spit it out. My mother had yelled at him and I remembered how he had laughed at her, saying it wouldn't hurt me.

He made awkward small talk in the dimly lit interior of the bus. "Well, how'd you do in school? Did you make good grades?"

I paused before I answered him; these were questions I resented, because if he'd been more of a part of my life, he would have known the answers. I toyed with the idea of telling him a bold-faced lie, saying I made straight A's and was the smartest kid in the class.

But I just mumbled "I guess," then shrugged him off and turned to look out the window into the darkness. In the window's reflection I saw his head turn away and his chin drop down as he stared at the floor in front of him. He looked terribly sad, but somehow it didn't bother me. After a few miles, I turned toward him and asked "What time do we stop again?" He had the schedule in the inside pocket of his jacket and as he reached for it, he saw my eyes rest on the bottle.

"You know, sometimes a man just needs a drink! This was hard for me—coming back to get you. Your mother could have had me arrested and thrown in jail. I took a big chance to do this!" His angry defense frightened me, yet I also felt a stab of undeserved compassion. I had forgotten that because of the nonpayment of child support there was a warrant out for him in Ohio.

My mind jumped back and forth between the past and the present. I noticed his stutter, and then remembered it from years ago. I noticed the way he wiped the tobacco juice from the corner of his mouth, then remembered it from years ago. I remembered he was always fastidious about his clothes, slapping my mother because of a wrinkle found in an ironed shirt. My mind stumbled over this, trying to imagine something as small as a wrinkle upsetting him when we were so poor we had nothing to eat. Then I remembered the drinking, the arguments, the violence and constant disruption of our lives. Once again I turned away from him and instead of watching his pitiful reflection in the window; I closed my eyes and slept.

At our next stop, we sat beside each other, eating our meal in silence. I abruptly got up and announced I was going to the ladies' room. I waited to wash my hands and face, watching women as they stood in front of the mirrors, their cigarettes balanced on the edges of the sinks while they applied another layer of lipstick and sprayed their already cemented hair. The polluted air choked me.

When it was finally my turn, I combed my hair back into a ponytail and splashed water on my face. The loud floral clothes my aunt gave me transformed my appearance from looking like I'd just jumped off a hay wagon to that of a hippie flower child. I stared in the bathroom mirror, trying to get used to my reflection. I kind of liked the new me. I deliberately took my time, knowing my father was waiting for me. I had no idea where we were, just a dot on the map, and I wondered if he felt the same uneasiness I did; if he regretted the whole idea of our trip together. Feeling a little refreshed, I strolled out and looked for a newsstand. I was reading magazines when my father came up behind me.

"I couldn't find you! Now you need to stay close to me—you don't know the kind of people who hang around places like this," he warned.

His bossiness irritated me, I wasn't a little kid anymore and I resented his late attempt at parenting. We'd managed just fine without him all these years. I thumped the magazine back in the rack and looked up at him. That's when I noticed how grey his eyes were. I had always thought they were green, like mine.

Maybe he really wasn't my father; he was some stranger taking me across the country. My father had thick brown hair and was taller and thinner, he had smiling eyes, even if I didn't remember the color, and a quick, hearty laugh. My father never hovered over us, nor protected us with his presence in a crowded place; instead he would throw us a dollar and tell us to get out of whatever bar he was in. We'd roam the streets well after the dime stores and movie theaters closed, then seek a place to sleep, usually the car or an empty pool table, until he drunkenly drove us home.

These thoughts haunted me as I clutched his jacket again, following him through the crowd to the outer doors.

A couple of days into the trip I grew tired of being confined to my seat. My clothes were rumpled, and the new fabric felt stiff and scratchy. The diesel smell stung my sinuses, and my ears roared from the noisy air conditioner. My father continued to chew tobacco, spit the juice in the paper cup, and take sips from his
106

hidden bottle. Every few miles he'd turn to me and speak, like it took him all that time to think of something. I wondered if any of it was the truth.

He told me he had a daughter who was ten but she wasn't his child; her father had died in a drowning accident. Her mother was of Indian descent and she reminded him of my mother, with her dark eyes and fiery temper. I remembered his insults to my own mother during their fights, calling her an Indian because her father was half Cherokee. I tried to shake this memory to concentrate on what he was saying. There was also a grown son and uncle who stayed at the house. I mentally counted the bedrooms, I thought he'd said three, and then I counted all the people and wondered where everyone slept. This bothered me.

He looked down at my sandals. "Did you bring any other shoes with you?" I stared down at my feet as I shook my head. He laughed and said "Well, we need to get you some shoes! There's a boot store downtown—maybe you'd like a pair of boots." I looked back out the window. I didn't want any boots. I remembered the shoes my aunt and uncle bought us at the beginning of every school year. By summer they were worn out and too small, so we went barefoot until school started again. I couldn't recall my father ever buying us shoes.

The more my father drank, the more he seemed to relax, and the more he relaxed, the more he talked. He confessed he met a woman in Idaho shortly after he arrived out west and he married her. He laughed as he said he was drunk at the time and when he sobered up, he left her and the town. He said he didn't know what happened to her. I was shocked—was he still married to her?

He said he had worked on a survey crew in the northwest for a few years. It was grueling work standing and walking on mountainsides but he said he loved being out in the rugged outdoors and the pay was decent. In between good paying jobs, he said he picked apples east of the mountains during harvest season.

Until the past year, he had tended bar at the Fo'c'sle on Pine Street, down on the waterfront of Puget Sound. He now worked in a small machine shop a few blocks from where they lived. Their house sat on a hill overlooking the Sound and he said they could see Mt. Rainier on a clear day from their kitchen window. He told me about Snoqualmie Falls at Snoqualmie Pass and how it was the most beautiful place on earth, and that he wanted to take me there and show me the waterfall cascading in a long drop down the mountainside. He added in a somber voice that when he died, he wanted cremated and his ashes strewn over the falls. I couldn't even begin to imagine my father dying; he seemed invincible.

He laughed as he told me stories of friends who visited the house, and how he couldn't wait to introduce me to them. He said he loved the northwest, he'd never return to live in Southern Ohio again. He talked about his garden in their back yard which he tended every evening.

My thoughts flashed back to our old garden. The garden was cursed by Johnson grass that grew a foot overnight in the rich soil of Ohio's river valley. He would come home on Fridays after working away all week. The first thing he did was check that garden. It had to be perfect. No weeds, no grass, and freshly hoed. We usually failed the garden inspection, suffering painful consequences of which my mother bore the brunt.

One spring, he asked me to help plant seeds in the freshly tilled, dark soil. I held the bag of corn as he placed exactly three kernels in evenly-spaced holes in perfectly parallel rows. I bent over, and in doing so, tipped the bag and spilled the corn.

He went berserk and grabbed the bag from me. "I knew you'd spill them! You can't do a damn thing right! I'll do it myself—just get the hell out of here!" He kept cussing me as he frantically picked up the spilled kernels. I ran wailing to my mother.

His voice interrupted my thoughts when he said how much he loved the fresh air with the cleansing rains, the sweet smell of pine, and the salty pungent odor of the ocean. Suddenly, he stopped talking and I looked at him, noticing the serious look on his face.

"How's your mom?" he looked directly at me. I squirmed in my seat. Far be it for me to say she hated his guts and had been on a ten-year bitter rant about him. So, I left out the fact that she, like him, lived inside a bottle. Her excuse, which I thought was a
108

valid one, was that it helped her cope with the many burdens on her shoulders.

I just smiled and said "She's okay. She's worried about the war." He admitted he was worried about my brother, too. He said he missed us through all the years and that he was sorry how things turned out. He didn't explain his lack of keeping in touch, but he did say he had wished we'd written him back. I didn't respond; I didn't know of any letters.

I started talking about my horse. I pulled her picture from my purse and proudly showed it to him. He didn't return it but instead placed it carefully in his shirt pocket. I told him about my stepfather's dairy farm, the early hours, the unending chores, and the hard work involved. I didn't divulge that we were drowning in debt and the farm was falling apart from neglect. I babbled on. When I showed him pictures of my sister's babies, he chuckled about her "shotgun wedding" and smiled as he studied their little faces.

When I paused to take a breath, he would jump in with memories about the farm where he grew up, stories of my uncles and their mischief. I vividly remembered my grandparents' farm, he and my mother had left me there one summer for a very long visit. He told me of an old army buddy he had reconnected with, they had been in Italy and Africa together during WWII. As we talked, our words flew as fast as the miles. When I became drowsy, I no longer leaned against the window to sleep but instead rested my head on my father's shoulder.

In the Rockies, we had a couple of hours to kill before boarding the bus. He suggested taking a walk downtown. The sidewalks were made of wood; the store fronts still had the old western facades. We peeked through the windows of the darkened shops and saw riding gear, cowboy boots, and hats. A breeze gently swirled the dusty sand and sagebrush around. There were horses in a corral at the edge of town and we could hear them nickering.

Suddenly, I wanted to run from him and hide. I wanted to stay there forever to feel the heat of the day long after dark. I wanted to walk the board sidewalks, smell the leather in the western stores, and feel the soft breeze that blew the sagebrush. The sky was so close I felt I could reach up and touch the stars. A horse's whinny from the corral beckoned to me. This town that time forgot had such a strong pull on me that I was tempted to let the bus, and my father, go on without me.

My father's little flat bottle was empty, and he was looking for a liquor store,without luck. It must have been the altitude, but my mind was racing how to escape and hide as fast as his was trying to find another bottle. After awhile, we slowly walked in silence back to the bus station.

As we angled through the mountains in the early dark hours before dawn, the bus swerved sharply and nearly knocked everyone out of their seats. The whole bus was suddenly awake, asking what happened, and some were even yelling at the bus driver, who had pulled over and stopped. He stood up and announced to us he had swerved to avoid hitting an elk. As everyone looked out the windows, all they could see were their own reflections.

The bus started up again and slowly gained speed on the mountainous road. My father looked at me and I could see anger flash in his eyes. He kept looking at the bus driver then back at me. "You know, he fell asleep! He fell asleep! I watched him. He fell asleep and drove off the road! There was no elk. I was watching the road! The man is a liar!"

I looked at my father then up at the driver, hoping he wouldn't hear him. My father wouldn't stop; he was so angry he was half stuttering, half spitting, and half sputtering, "He could have killed us all. The man went to sleep and lied about it!"

I sighed, hoping my father would just get over it, but he wouldn't let it go. He sat up even straighter and diligently watched the road ahead, barely visible from the headlights of the bus. I stared out the side window. After awhile, I grew tired of seeing myself, so I closed my eyes and tried to sleep, but I could sense the anger from my father beside me. I sat up with him, watching the bus driver, watching the road, watching him watch the bus driver, watching the road. It was exhausting. We continued this vigil until dawn lightened the sky. My eyelids felt like crepe paper. I was sick of the bus, sick of being in the same hideous, and by then uncomfortable, clothes for how many days I didn't know, I had lost track in the blur of miles and rest stops. I was so miserable and tired at that point, I really didn't care if the bus did drive over the edge of the mountain. I agonized over meeting my father's family looking like I did. I no longer wanted to escape or run away. I just wanted to bathe and sleep in a bed.

After days and nights on a bus from Ohio to Washington, we finally arrived. We were waiting outside the Seattle bus station looking like two vagabonds when a white car pulled up to the curb. A dark-haired woman and cherub-faced little girl got out and hurried toward us.

My father waved and yelled "Well helloooo there!" I glanced at him and was surprised to see tears in his eyes. As the woman and little girl approached, he put his arm around my shoulder and pulled me close to his side, holding onto me in a tight grip. He nervously started to stutter and then his voice broke as he said, "I'd like you to meet—meet my daughter!"

I was stunned by his emotional introduction. I couldn't remember my father ever showing me any affection. Although I had only known him for a few days, I knew I wanted him to be my father. Whoever this stranger was, I wanted to go back in time with him and recapture those lost years. I wanted him to get in his truck and turn it around so that little girl could finally push the screen door open and run out of the house crying, "Daddy, Daddy, you came back!"

Peg Hanna

Peg Hanna, formally Margaret Leis Hanna, loves to play with words. Her signature for emails includes "Always Writing."

As an award winning author and poet she has always been writing. She began as a teen writing different endings for Nancy Drew novels.

An alumna of Grove City College (PA) with graduate work at the University of Pittsburgh, The Ohio State University and Highlights Foundation, Peg has published childrens books with Sprite Press (*The Blue Cap*, *Canneh the Reluctant Camel*, and *Seeing Stars*). She relied on years of experience as a first grade and middle school reading teacher to write eleven leveled readers for Zaner-Bloser Educational Publishers.

She is a member of the Ohio Writer's Guild, Franklinton Writers and Select Authors.

Peg recently co-authored *While...: Born During WWII*, which features contrasting memoirs of her life as Margaret Leis Hanna, an American, and Brunhilde Maurer Barron, a German, whom she met as an adult.

Peg is married, a mother to six and a grandmother of eight.

Visit her website, www.peg-board.net.

FROM EMPTY ENVELOPES
By Peg Hanna

"Don't go near her," Manny, one of the Sheffield Soup Kitchen gang called to the newcomer. "She'll write about you." He pointed to the woman seated at the last bench in the pale green former school cafeteria.

Wearing a long black overcoat, red sweat suit, scuffed army boots and white baseball cap, the stooped man shuffled towards the woman sitting alone in the corner of the cafeteria. Wisps of gray hair framed her bandana. Her eyes darted from table to table like windshield wipers.

"Always writin'," shouted Manny, a short man with shoulder-length black hair, who sat at a table in the middle of the cafeteria. "Licking that pencil stub, writing on old envelopes."

James, with a long nose like a weasel, looked up from his seat, "Her name's Rogene—rhymes with 'Go Green'." He snickered. "She's writing about us."

"Write about me today, Rogene. Got me a new boyfriend," taunted Birdie, with her bosom resting on the table top.

The newcomer threaded the aisles between long tables with attached benches and joined Rogene. He sat across from her, hurriedly filling his belly with watery beef stew, stale Valentine's Day cut-out cookies, and black coffee. When he'd finished, he stood and tipped his cap. "Need a smoke," he said and left.

"Rogene's alone again," Ron, who sported a salt and pepper beard, yelled. "Scared him off too!"

Suddenly, James sneaked up behind Rogene and pinched her, sending her upper body sprawling across the table and scattering her old envelopes across the table and the dirty linoleum floor. James scooped up the envelopes and held them high in the air. "Notes for sale! Find out what she wrote." The soup kitchen diners surrounded him and jumped up and down, begging like puppies. "What'll you give for notes about you?"

"I'll sing for mine," Ron said and jumped atop a nearby table.

In a raspy voice, he began "Oh when the saints go marchin' in . . ." The diners joined in, clapped, and marched around the table.

When they had finished, Birdie shouted, "I can do better. Lift me up, boys." When no one came to her aid, she hefted herself atop the Formica tabletop, lifted her skirts, and danced a lively Irish jig. Everyone whistled and cheered.

"A trick for mine," Manny shouted from another tabletop. Showing empty hands, he reached down and pulled a quarter from Ron's beard.

"Hey," Ron shouted. "Where did you get that? I didn't have no money!"

James distributed each performer's notes as if they were dollar bills.

Meanwhile, in the corner, Rogene hobbled towards the door without a word, bumping into the returning newcomer.

"Rogene's goin' to the dumpster for more writin' paper!" Ron shouted. The diners erupted in laughter.

The newcomer followed Rogene out into March sunlight.

"My name's Sheridan," he said, tipping his cap. "I used to be a boxer, but I lost some important things too."

"I'm Rogene," she replied. "Thanks for the company. Wanna come to the library with me?"

"Nah, I'm heading over to Norm's gym. I'll sweep up, punch a few bags and kick out the punks."

When she entered the library, Rogene heard Marie, one of the librarians, call her name. "Rogene, I saved you some envelopes."

Rogene shook her head, stumbled into the restroom, and slumped into a heap in a corner. She stared at the mint-green tiles beneath her scuffed, dirty sneakers, and considered her path to this place. Once a meticulous dresser, she now wore a green and blue plaid skirt over torn blue jeans, a button-less yellow cardigan, and layers of sweaters to keep out the late winter chill.

A soft knock on the door interrupted Rogene's thoughts and Marie tiptoed into the restroom. "Why aren't you at your usual table? What happened, Rogene?"

"It's all gone," Rogene muttered. "My mother, my job, my house, and now my notes."

Marie kneeled down beside her. "What do you mean?"

Rogene spoke softly, her eyes still glued to the floor. "I cared for my mother for more than ten years, and I took over the payments on her house when she died. I trusted the wrong mortgage broker. It all disappeared so quickly after I was laid off—twenty-three years as a department head. I couldn't pay the bills and the bank foreclosed on the house." Her voice shook as tears flowed. It was the first time she'd really told her story. She took a deep breath and continued. "I registered with a job search organization. They gave me a thumb drive to store my resume, but I haven't had one call, one email. I always wanted to write a story, and I started, but I lost my notes today."

Marie laid her hand on Rogene's arm. "I can tell by the way you talk that you're educated. Why are you living like this?"

"I have no choice. I have no credentials. I'm good enough with computers, but I don't have a college degree or experience in anything other than what I spent the last twenty years doing. I'm fifty-five—with no recommendations, address, or phone, who'd want to hire me?"

A loud vibration interrupted and Marie pulled her phone from her pocket and glanced at the screen. "I'm sorry, Rogene, I have to get back to the desk. Let me know if there's anything I can do to help. You know you can always use the library computers."

"Yeah, but it costs money for print-outs," Rogene mumbled.

Marie didn't seem to hear her. She opened the door and turned back to face Rogene. "I'll check in with you before I punch out and go home."

The word punch stayed with Rogene. She put her head on her arms. PUNCH! Where had she heard that word before? "Sheridan!" she said to the walls, "If Sheridan can clean a gym and punch gym equipment, I can clean an office and punch a computer keyboard."

She washed her face, ventured into the library, and found a

115

want ad in the newspaper for nighttime cleaning persons for the newspaper offices. She asked Marie for phone money, called, and was told to report that night. They're as desperate as I am, Rogene thought.

During the first week of cleaning, Rogene slept mornings in the library or bus station and ate lunch at the soup kitchen. She could shower in the company locker room now—no more sneaking into the city fountain at night. After a few days, James yelled from his usual seat in the soup kitchen, "Haven't seen you at the shelter, Rogene." He winked. "Doin' night tricks?"

Rogene carried her cold spaghetti and soggy salad past him without responding. Heading for her corner, she scanned the tables for Sheridan.

Birdie sidled up next to her. "Collected your 'lopes from the other day," she whispered. She retrieved the folded envelopes from the "V" of her pink, moth-eaten sweater. "Here," she said, putting them on Rogene's tray. "I can't read 'em anyway."

Standing in line, Manny called, "You're looking happy today, Rogene."

"Writing about someone else?" Ron shouted from his usual table.

Back at her table, Birdie threw down her fork and stood up, put her hands on her hips and hollered. "Leave her alone, boys."

Rogene gave Birdie a smile, spied Sheridan walking in, and waved. He approached her table and tipped his hat, "Lookin' good, girl."

"I got a job, got my notes back," Rogene said. "I'm working on a new story. Can I write about you?"

"Me?" Sheridan stumbled. His coffee sloshed onto his tray.

Rogene nodded. "I can use the computers now."

Sheridan frowned. "Who'd want to read about me—I ain't nothing but a worn out boxer."

"Everybody, you'll see. I have a place to type your story."

Sheridan tossed his white cap in the air. "I might be famous yet."

116

Bumping desks as she cleaned the newspaper offices, Rogene found one computer asleep—someone had forgotten to log out. She spread her envelopes on the desk, slipped in her thumb drive, and opened up her story. She'd spent hours typing at the library, telling the story of the lightweight Navy contender. Discharged, with no one to fight, he'd hit the bottle and the streets. She paused to read over the final paragraph for a moment, then hit "print."

Without warning, a patrolling security guard entered the office. "What are you doing?" He strode towards her. "You're not a reporter. You're not allowed to use this computer."

In one motion, he swept her envelopes off the desk. "I have to report you to your supervisor. Anything printed in this office must be reported to Mr. Kramer, the editor." The guard grabbed the print-out and read part of the story. "Mr. Kramer needs to know what a cleaning lady does on the clock."

Rogene grabbed his arm. "Please, don't report me."

The guard shook free. He looked at Rogene's badge and scribbled her name at the top of the paper in his hand.

Rogene persisted, "Please, I can't lose my job."

The guard turned and walked away. "I'm just doing my job."

"Please, just let me have that print-out." Rogene pleaded. "People need to hear this story. I have nowhere else to print it."

He started out the door shaking his head. "Cleaning lady thinks she's a reporter . . . "

Rogene slumped over the keyboard. Now I've lost one more thing, she thought. She spun around in her chair and kicked her supply cart, sending it rolling down the aisle, where it crashed into the wall and spilled bottles and rags all over the floor. Rogene turned her back to the cleaning supplies and shouted to the man leaving the room, "Go ahead—report me!" She pocketed her thumb drive, retrieved her cart and its contents and pushed it out of the room.

The following night as she cleaned Kramer's office, Rogene checked the editor's desk for her story. Maybe she could find the manuscript before he could. One Monday night, Rogene saw Sheridan's story on the desk. A note attached read: "I want to see this person at 8 a.m. Wednesday morning."

Tuesday night Rogene saw a note posted on her locker: "Report to Mr. Kramer's office at 8 a.m. Wednesday morning".

"That's the end of my shift!" she shouted.

With every mop stroke that night she imagined the interview. Rogene needed to defend herself. She had no references, no decent clothes other than her uniform. She wondered if this would be her last night at the newspaper. What would she say? How would she explain how her story got to Kramer's desk?

With no time to change, Rogene had to meet the editor in her uniform: a gray T-shirt, black slacks, and black shoes. She washed her face, fluffed her hair, pinched her cheeks, and knocked on the editor's door.

"Come in," Kramer said. His back was to Rogene when she opened the door, but he swiveled around to face her. "Oh, my office has already been cleaned, thank you."

"Mr. Kramer, you asked to see me." Rogene straightened her back. "I'm Rogene Stone. I was reported for using the computers."

He looked her up and down. "But you're the cleaning lady!" he blurted.

"I wrote the story about the homeless boxer," Rogene said.

He picked up the manuscript. "I guess it says 'by Rogene Stone'." He paused and scanned the document again. "This is great insight into the man's character."

"Thank you." Rogene approached his desk. "Mr. Kramer, I can write another story with just as much insight as Sheridan's."

Kramer stared at her. "Okay," he said slowly. He tapped his pencil on his desk. "Write me another story by Friday at noon."

Rogene nodded. "I have a series about the homeless in mind. I'll drop a story off after work."

"Where do you work?"

Rogene looked at her feet and mumbled, "Here."

Kramer stared at her again. "And you plan to use a company computer?" He reshuffled papers on his desk. "Right. I have a report on that, too." He glanced at her story again. "Your story is well-

118

written. You deserve your own computer. I'll have one available for you."

Two weeks later, Rogene rushed into the soup kitchen, newspaper in hand, asking for Sheridan. The regulars sat in their usual spots.

"I didn't recognize you without your bandana," Manny said.

"And you're wearing clean jeans and a nice sweatshirt," Birdie added.

Rogene smiled. "I got a job and I'm saving money for a place to stay. And I even have a computer to use." She looked around the area. "Where's Sheridan? Want to read him his story in today's paper. He's the first in my series."

"Sheridan hasn't been around," Ron said, shaking his head. He patted the bench next to him. "Sit here. Read it to us."

Rogene sat, unfolded the newspaper and read the headline:

"FORMER BOXER NOW FIGHTS POVERTY, by Rogene Stone."

Birdie slipped onto the bench beside her. "Sheridan's gone, girl." She put her arm around Rogene.

James wiped his nose and stood. "They found him dead by the gym."

Rogene lowered her head.

"Don't cry, girl." Birdie reached over and pulled Rogene's head to her bosom. "You made him famous, like he wanted."

Manny sat down across from them. "You gotta keep writin' Rogene," he said. "Lord knows there's more stories in the Sheffield Soup Kitchen." He reached into his pocket, and laid an empty envelope on the table in front of her.

Catherine Maynard

The main character of the fictional story "Dead Man's Daughter" did not die in her car accident, but some things did: her hearing, her spirit, and her family relationships.

Catherine would like to thank Jim and Beth Maynard for supporting her through every edit, every contest, every convention, every weird writer's quirk, and for letting her wander the hallways and haunt the rooms of their house until 0400 on any given day.

She would also like to thank Seth, Becky, and Rachel for being the only people who can tolerate her (and still love her) when she's in the middle of an important scene.

Catherine studied French at Ohio University (another thanks here to Dr. Vines, Dr. Toner, and the rest of the French department in Gordy Hall, who gave her the time and understanding she so desperately needed). She has lived and studied in Quebec, France, and Germany, and plans to attend graduate school in either France or Germany and specialize in 20th and 21st Century French Literature.

Catherine plans to earn her doctorate and teach, but has always been (and always will be) a writer. She once asked her father how long he thought it would take to "become a real writer." He responded: "You're already a real writer. The question isn't about you; the question's about how long it takes for the rest of the world to catch on."

Find more of her work, and contact her via her website, cynicalinsomniac.tumblr.com.

DEAD MAN'S DAUGHTER
By Catherine Maynard

I knew the pianist was playing "Amazing Grace" because that's what it said in the program. I knew the priest was saying kind words and praises, but I'll never know exactly what he said. No one thought to get an interpreter for the dead man's daughter. Why would they? Even I was a little surprised to find myself sitting in a rigid church pew. He'd been dead to me for years; I was long done mourning.

I didn't cry. I knew my mother was crying hysterically, but I couldn't hear her sobs. Sometimes being deaf has its advantages.

I've become used to simply *watching*, and I was content to do so that day. I didn't mind sitting in my own world of silence and watching the funeral unfold like a play around me, watching the characters enter from stage left or right. Priest, enter stage left, costumed in a black robe and a white collar. Altar boy, enter stage right, head obediently bowed and face appropriately solemn. Spotlight on the closed casket in the middle of the stage, adorned with flowers and a picture of a man I no longer knew.

I watched my mother play the bereaved widow, sobbing hysterically into a kerchief. I watched my brother hold her hand in an absent way, checking his watch every six or seven minutes. I watched my teenage niece surreptitiously check her cell phone for text messages from her new boyfriend. Finding none, she slipped the phone back into her purse and stared ahead with bored determination.

We weren't sitting together, my family and I. I didn't dare. That would have made an already uncomfortable situation completely unbearable for all of us.

The priest said something that sent my mother into gales of hysteria, clutching her Bible desperately against her chest. For the second time in as many minutes I was happy I couldn't hear her.

121

My brother seemed completely overwhelmed. He grabbed both of her hands and spoke to her in what I assumed was a whisper. He was the kind of man who never liked to make a scene.

My niece's face reddened in embarrassment and she placed her head in her hands. But she couldn't have been too upset; after a few seconds she slipped her phone out of her purse, pushed a button, sighed discontentedly, and returned the phone to its home.

Suddenly everyone's heads turned toward the side of the church. A man's hand dashed into his pocket, his face red and his mouth saying, "I'm sorry." I couldn't hear the ringtone, but I knew it was loud and obnoxious, because even the priest stopped talking for a moment. Soon everyone turned back to the front and the priest started again.

The church was brimming with people I had never met. Most of them seemed sincere enough, but some were obviously there for appearances. Still, I respect anyone who can sit in a sweltering church for an hour on a Saturday afternoon, no matter how selfish the motivations.

There was one exception: an older man on the other side of the church, toward the back. I've become adept at observing people over the years, and this man was somehow different from everyone else. I didn't know him and I didn't know how he knew my father, but I was immediately curious. I made a mental note to take my notepad with me and talk to him at the wake.

I glanced at my watch. The funeral would be over soon and then we would have to go to the graveside service. I've never understood why we need, essentially, two funeral services. Doesn't one do? And what's the point of a wake? A wake is just an excuse for everyone to use the line "I'm sorry" a million different times and not mean it once.

In any language, in almost any situation, those words mean nothing. "I'm sorry" usually means "I don't know what else to say." Or—more often than one would think—it means, "I'm so glad it wasn't me."

Like after my accident. So many people uttered the words "I'm sorry," and they meant less and less every time I heard them—well, saw them. I lost my hearing somewhere between the steering wheel and the headrest. Gone, in the time it took for my brain to slosh around in my skull as my head rebounded. I suffered a cut on my forehead, a broken arm, a dislocated shoulder, and my hearing was destroyed.

Nothing. Total silence.

I was seventeen.

They praised me for wearing my seatbelt, because otherwise I might be dead. They told me that I was lucky a cop was driving by, because otherwise I might be dead. They told me to look on the bright side, because it could have been much worse.

No one knew that for months after the crash I wished I hadn't worn my seatbelt. I wished that the cop had just stayed away. I wished for it to be worse, just so I wouldn't have to deal with the never-ending silence.

A few weeks after the accident I remember a nurse holding my hand as I cried. I remember watching her mouth say the words, "I'm sorry." That was the first time I was ever glad that I couldn't hear.

My mother and father separated after the accident; it was the "straw that broke the camel's back," they told me. My mother stopped trying to talk to me. She didn't try to draw me out of my room. She didn't try to help me. She fed me, she bought me clothes, she paid for my hospital bills.

My brother lived in another state, and with almost fifteen years between our ages, we were never close.

My dad moved out.

I moved out, too, a few weeks later, on the day I turned eighteen.

I hated them. While I was learning ASL I offered to teach

them and they declined. My mom didn't give me a reason for her refusal; my dad said he just didn't have the time. That seemed worse, like he couldn't make time for me because I was broken. It didn't take long to let him go, let him die in my mind.

The funeral service finally ended, and the priest held up his hands and said something as the altar boy took his place. My mother clutched her Bible in one hand and my brother's arm in her other as she shakily gained her feet.

I hadn't seen my mother in two years and I was surprised by how old she looked. Her naturally Irish-red hair was turning grey at the temples. Wrinkles—not laugh lines, certainly—etched themselves into her forehead and beside her eyes. I couldn't tell if she was frowning or if her lips naturally turned that way after years of practice.

She glided out of the church on my brother's arm without looking my way. I don't know if she saw me, but it didn't matter. She wouldn't have recognized my presence even if I sat next to her during the service. As she'd told me before, she just didn't know how to talk to me without being awkward.

I filed out of my pew with everyone else and made my way to the door. It was cooler outside than inside the church, a slight breeze rustling through the old trees lining the churchyard, the bright sun shining down from a cloudless sky.

I lifted my face to the sky and let the sun warm my skin. Despite the circumstances, I was feeling good. I felt . . . closure. I thought I could go back to school, pop in a movie, and move on with my life.

Someone bumped into me from behind and I automatically turned and signed, "Sorry." Why is it that when someone bumps into you, *you* feel the urge to apologize?

It was the man I'd noticed earlier, the older man with the blue eyes and kind face. As I started walking to the parking lot, I felt him following me. I picked up my pace, not wanting to get into the

124

ever awkward "I can't hear you" charade. He stayed right on my heels. Just as I was about to turn and get it over with he touched my shoulder. I turned, ready to mimic "I'm deaf."

Instead of speaking, he signed, "You're Valerie, right?"

I didn't respond, I just tilted my head curiously and nodded.

He signed, "I'm Mark. I was a friend of your father's." His signing was fluid and fast; he was obviously fluent. We shook hands and then he signed, "I'm so sorry about your dad."

For some reason his words felt *real*, but I still responded the way I'd planned: "Thanks, but we weren't very close."

Mark's eyebrows shot up and he frowned. "Really?"

"How did you know my father?"

"I only knew him for a few months, but he seemed like a really good guy. And it's surprising to hear you weren't close. He talked about you all the time in class."

I repeated, *"Class?"*

Mark looked at me, my expression of confusion mirrored on his face. "ASL class," he signed slowly. "I was his teacher. He started a few months ago; he said he finally had the time to learn it. And he talked about you all the time." Then, "He didn't tell you?"

I shook my head as it sunk in. I felt numb. Tears stood in my eyes. ASL classes. For me. To talk to me. I felt a single tear slide down my cheek.

"I'm so sorry. I thought you knew. I didn't mean to upset you."

I shook my head again, waving his apology away. *"I'm fine."* I tried a smile but it felt false. My mind was reeling, but I kept returning to one thing. Two weeks ago. An email. An offer to buy me dinner.

Mark was signing at me but I wasn't watching. Suddenly I interrupted him. "I'm sorry, I have to go."

He said, "Of course. The burial. I'll see you there."

But I didn't go to the graveside service. I drove around for hours, the road a watery blur beneath the tires. I realized vaguely that I was driving away from where I needed to go, but I didn't care.

My mind kept going back to the email, the last correspondence I'd ever had from my father.

> Val—
>
> *Sorry we haven't talked much recently. But I'll be on your side of town tonight, around six. Dinner on me? I want to talk to you.*
>
> *-Dad*

There it was again, usually so nonchalant and empty. "Sorry."

But the words that had seemed so unimportant before now stuck in my mind in all capitals.

SORRY.

TALK TO YOU.

I had deleted the email without responding. Had he waited for my reply? Was he excited to show me what he'd learned?

I want to talk to you.

Why didn't I go? Why didn't I at least respond or send him a text?

Four years. Four years since I had heard my father's voice. Four years since any significant communication essentially ended; only the occasional email or text message broke the silence.

I want to talk to you, he'd written.

And I clicked *Delete* without a second thought.

I don't know how long I drove. But it was dark when I finally parked at the cemetery. The service was long over; the cemetery was still and empty.

I walked through the valley of graves and stopped when I saw a freshly dug rectangle of earth.

I felt my throat utter the word "Dad" as I fell to my knees.

Tears dripped from my chin and onto the fresh flowers littering the grave.

Then suddenly I started signing. I was desperate to talk to him—really *talk* to him, like he'd wanted to. He felt alive to me for the first time in years, so I held my end of the conversation we should have had. I told him about my life. I told him how much I miss him. I told him that I love him. I told him I'd come back soon, with flowers. And then, before I walked back to my car and drove away, I touched the little white cross marking his grave and signed, "I'm sorry."

Birney Reed

Education: Yes, he has one, or most of one. He had two quarters to go before he quit The Ohio State University to pursue a life lived hard and well.

Employment: Former jack of all trades and absolute master of none.

The story "Rerun" you are about to read is an unusual tale written with just one question in mind. "What would you do if you could live your life over again?"

Birney has some thanking to do here.

1. His wife (she told him he had to thank her and like a smart man he agreed with her), he's been married twenty-three years and the woman deserves a medal for it.

2. Brad Pauquette, he saw the premise of this story and encouraged Birney to work with it. Birney will be eternally grateful for his advice, guidance and editorial skills.

3. Terry Lonergan and John Rose, the two best friends a man can have.

If you have read all of this, you're either starving for the printed word or you're just plain nosey. Either way works for Birney.

Please enjoy reading "Rerun" as much as Birney enjoyed writing it.

RERUN

By Birney Reed

I dreamed that I was in my own bed, in my own room, with my leviathan of a wife lying next to me. I was looking down at myself and up at the ceiling at the same time. Suddenly, my heart stopped. It wasn't a sensation, and it wasn't painful. Something stopped, something that had been constant, as if I were lying in the grass on an Ohio summer night, and suddenly, all of the crickets stopped at once, and for the first time in my life, silence penetrated my mind. The dream felt so real, that if it weren't so absurd, I would have sworn I was awake. As the blood lay stagnant in my veins and pooled in my arteries, I could feel my body grow cold and rigid. I felt released, like a satisfying belch, and I watched as my lips turned blue.

Suddenly, I was standing in the middle of a forest I had played in as a kid. It wasn't much of a forest—just a clump of trees with a runoff flowing through it in the middle of the city. But, when I was a child, this little patch of wilderness was as vast and empty as Sherwood Forest.

The woods smelled sweet and clean. Small twigs and old leaves, covering the forest floor, made a swishing sound as my red Hi-Top Keds disturbed their rest. My heart was pounding, not out of fear but pure joy. It was the joy of being alive. I blinked and the dream blew away.

I awakened next to my wife, Carol. I felt alive and refreshed, like a medicine ball had finally been lifted off of my chest after forty years. Carol was lying in the gully that was her side of the bed. In the magic of the morning light, I thought maybe she would look as young as I felt. She jumped when I reached over and my mission came back with nothing but a handful of sweaty back fat.

"What the . . . " she shrieked.

"Sorry, sweetheart," I muttered. I was a sixty-year-old man; it would have taken more than that woman's morbid obesity to cool me off on the day once a quarter when I could actually get heated up.

"Sweetheart? Why the hell you calling me that?" The bed rattled on its cheap steel rails as she heaved her body over to face me. She took one look at me. If it wasn't for her eyes, her face might have been funny. Terror occupied her eyes. She jumped out of bed like they were giving away Haagen Daz in the hallway, and I heard her run to the kitchen and dump all of the silverware on the floor. The change on my dresser rattled as she hustled her heft back down the hallway.

As soon as she came back into the room, she thrust the knife in my direction and screamed, "What did you do with my husband, you fucking punk?"

"Carol?" I tried to soothe her. "What the hell are you doing?"

"What did you do with him you piece of shit? Why are you in my house?" Confusion gripped her face and she waved the knife back and forth like she was harvesting wheat.

"Your house? This is my house. Carol, get your shit together!"

"GET-GET-GET OUT OF MY HOUSE!" she stammered, and reached for the phone on her nightstand. She dialed 9-1-1 as I looked on incredulously.

"Screw this," I muttered, threw on a pair of pants, grabbed my keys and wallet from the dresser and headed for the front door.

My wife had snapped before. It was best to head down the road to Plank's on Parsons Avenue when she went menopausal. Darting out the back door, I tripped over my pants as they fell down around my ankles, and my face smacked the crumbling asphalt driveway. Carol's shrill voice was moving closer to the door.

I pulled up my pants, yanked the belt way past the last notch in the leather and tucked it back over itself, and jumped in our rust bucket. Carol came running after me and I could hear her telling the police, "He's stealing my car! The son of a bitch is stealing my car!"

It was 9:30 Saturday morning, I'd only been awake a few minutes, and the absurdity of what was happening didn't register in my mind, so I just drove off with the image of her coming at me with the butcher knife burned in my mind. I decided Carol had gone off the deep end.

Every town has a Plank's. It's a neighborhood tavern that serves double shots of bar well whiskey with its scrambled eggs in the morning. The eggs are just a garnish to give the alcoholics an excuse to get started early.

"Hey Tony, give me a double," I shouted at the barkeep as I sank my ass down on a stool. It wasn't the first time I'd seen Tony so early in the morning.

The pockmarked face of the heavyset bartender reading the paper down at the end of the bar turned in my direction. "A double of what, kid?"

"Just give me the goddamn drink so I can tell you about it, Tony!"

He got off his stool and walked down to where I was sitting. "What'll you have?"

"Tony, if my hand is still empty in ninety seconds, I swear I might punch you in the face."

"Look, punk! What do you want before I throw you out on your ass?"

"Whiskey, Tony! Whiskey."

One shake of a leg later, Tony set whiskey in front of me and stood there. I handed him a five and told him to get one for himself. A second later two singles were sitting in front of me. That's when I caught my reflection in the smoke-caked mirror. My whiskey went crashing to the scarred bar top as my hand spasmed with surprise. A young man, about twenty-five, looked back at me with fresh color in his cheeks. I looked at his mouth, thin lips and

131

dark day-old stubble, then moved to his nose, smooth and straight, untouched by cheap shots in drunken brawls. The only thing I recognized were those eyes. Those were my eyes.

The world turned in on me and suddenly I was staring at the oak paneled ceiling above the bar, laying flat on my back on the floor. I struggled to sit up. Tony was looking down on me from behind the bar. "Hey kid, I never even touched you, so don't you go calling the cops!"

This wasn't a dream; my head was throbbing from its impact with the hardwood floor. But at the same time, my thoughts were clearer than they had been in years, I imagined gunk being stripped out of my neural pathways, tar and debris peeling away like in those engine additive commercials. I stood up, rubbed my head and saw my reflection in the mirror again. The kid in the glass was rubbing his head too.

"Tony, I gotta go," I mumbled.

"You're damn right you do!" he yelled at my back as I stumbled out of the bar.

Back in the daylight, a cop car was pulling in behind my rust bucket. I owned the piece of shit outright, but the image in the bar mirror didn't look anything like the picture on my driver's license and Lord knows what my wife had told the police, so I spun on my heels and headed in the other direction.

Walking seemed like the thing to do. During my stroll to nowhere, I stopped several times to stare at my reflection in the storefront windows. Each time I became more accustomed to the person looking back at me. My double chin was gone, along with my belly. The young man in the storefront glass was filled with the juice of life.

I thought about going home. But then I looked in those eyes of mine, full of life and clarity, and I heard the bed groan every time Carol rolled over, and I imagined her swinging that knife at me.

"There are so many other places a young man like me could be," I laughed out loud.

I don't know how far I walked, and I don't know if I was looking for a hospital or a college bar, but the chill of the evening came crashing down hard and I found myself looking through the window of a Denny's. A tight bodied, honey-blond waitress, with a face that told of a hard life, set a stack of steaming pancakes in front of a dour looking old woman. My hand went to my pocket feeling for the remainder of my paycheck. I pulled out the pitiful wad of bills and counted eighty-three bucks. The cost of the pancakes looked about right. Blondie caught me staring at her through the glass and smiled. The smile told me if I played my cards right, the cakes would be free, along with anything else I wanted.

The rich smell of brewing coffee stirred me to consciousness. I rolled over on my side and looked around the room, which was filled with frilly doilies. From down the hall I heard Lisa's hard West Virginia hillbilly twang pierce the air. "You want some coffee, sugar?"

I knew instantly that what I wanted was to get the hell out of there. It was time to move down the road and forget this little rendezvous of pleasure with the hash slinger from Denny's. I walked out to the kitchen. Lisa was wearing a baby doll apron and nothing else.

"Hey, baby! Could I stay the day, until I get my bearings?"

She smiled at me and answered, "Sugar, you can stay the week if you like. I haven't had lovin' like that since my old man left me. By the way, he left some clothes behind. They might fit you, yours are just way too big for you."

Lisa turned, brushed her lush body up against mine, looked up and smiled. I noticed the black decaying teeth on the right side of her lower jaw. This woman will rot away before my eyes, I thought.

That morning I sat and ate fried eggs, trying to make up my mind whether I'd just stuffed a woman fifteen years younger than me, or twenty years my senior. I didn't like either answer.

Two days later, I was on a bus heading south out of Columbus, Ohio, with the song "Hello Life, Goodbye Columbus" playing in my mind. I'd seen the movie *Midnight in the Garden of Good and Evil* once and liked the look of Savannah. With five hundred dollars in my pocket, which was everything I could find in Lisa's house, and several pairs of new jeans, T-shirts and socks jammed into a duffle bag, the image of Lisa's rotting teeth faded in my mind. The four Xanex I put in her orange juice guaranteed she'd sleep for at least twenty-four hours so I could make my getaway. I leaned back in the seat and immediately fell asleep.

"Savannah! Twenty minutes!" shouted the driver.

I opened my eyes to see the flat marshland of southeast Georgia. I stepped off the air-conditioned bus into humidity so thick it felt like I was breathing water. A bum resting on the curb just outside the terminal looked up at me and spoke. "You new to town, boy?"

"Who you calling boy . . . " I started to say, then caught myself. "Where can a guy get a room and something to eat?"

"Cost you a buck, stranger."

I reached down and grabbed the wino's greasy ear, twisting hard. "You'll tell me what I want to know, old-timer, or I'll rip off your head and shit down your neck!"

"Ow! You rotten son of a bitch! " He screamed as I twisted harder, "The Southern just around the corner'll give you a room for fifteen a night and any fast food restaurant'll give you a cheap meal."

I had no intention of taking his advice, but it felt good to force it out of him. A flea bag hotel and crappy food wasn't what I wanted. I wanted the good life. I let go of his ear, walked by a trashcan and threw my wallet in with the other refuse of the day. It was a fitting burial for the beaten down man known as Timothy Ripley. I was a newborn with no name.

Years of living had taught me a few things. I asked a couple walking some type of pedigree dog with dyed pink fur where the better eateries were in town. As luck would have it, the best places were within five blocks of the very hotel the old drunk had recommended.

One hour later, I had a new job and a new name. The application asked for name, address, phone number, of course there was a place for references. I faked them all. I was Joseph Leary (please don't call me Joe), the new waiter at the 606 Café. The name would do until I could get one better suited to the new me. Marcy, the manager, liked the name Joseph and she sure liked me. She gave "fraternization with the help" a whole new meaning. After a hard day's work, I spent the night at her place, and took a long hot shower after she left the next morning to open for the lunch rush. I headed to the county courthouse.

"Mr. Grimes, here's your birth certificate. Please try to store your documents in a safe place. In this day and age it's too easy for someone to steal your identification. Why just the other day . . . "

It shouldn't have been so simple, but all I had to do was go to the cemetery and find someone who died at birth about twenty-five years ago. Then I went to the county seat, asked for a duplicate birth certificate (death records are rarely kept in the same place), then beat feet to Social Security to order a card. A number had never been applied for, so they issued one. I walked out of the Savannah Courthouse as Paul Andrew Grimes.

I knew that the paperwork takes years to catch up.

Work that night was a breeze. As the evening wound down, a beautiful long-haired redhead sat down at one of my tables. I'd already been cut for the evening, but I figured I'd get her something to drink.

I sauntered up to Red, as I began to call her in my mind, admiring the way her expensive knee-length black dress hugged every curve. "Your server'll be over in a moment, can I get you something to drink?" rolled out of my mouth in the best Southern drawl I could fake.

Her blue-green eyes scanned me from the bottom of my shoes to the top of my head. The next sentence out of her mouth terrified me to my bones. "Do you plan on killing her before you leave or are you just going to disappear in the night?"

"Huh?" was my intelligent answer.

What she did next knocked me off my mental feet. She slithered out of the chair, brushing against my body on the way up, grabbed me behind the neck. Her tongue counted every tooth in my head. She stepped back, smiled and headed out the side door.

Marcy's gravelly voice rang out behind me "Who the hell was that?"

I didn't turn to look at her, "I don't have a clue . . . "

The rest of my night turned to shit. Two questions repeated themselves, over and over. Who was she? How did she know I was going to rip Marcy off and bolt? I still stayed at Marcy's place that night, but she didn't get any. It's hard for a man to get it up when fear has gripped his spine. As the sun began to rise, sleep finally reached me. The striking redhead filled my slumber, chasing me through thorn bushes that raked my skin like tiny razor blades. "Red," with her perfectly manicured nails, scratched and clawed at me. I woke up screaming.

The shadows on the wall told me it was late afternoon. I swung my feet out of bed, and landed in something liquid and sticky on the floor. The room smelled like mineral salts and iron. I muttered "What the hell?" as I raised my left foot to figure out what had spilled on the floor. In the half-light of the bedroom I could make out a raggedy looking ball at the foot of the bed. My hands slammed over my mouth to stifle the vomit bursting from my throat as I stared down at the dead eyes of Marcy's decapitated head. On the other side of the bed rested Marcy's twitching body trunk. Blood was still spurting from her headless neck.

I hear it takes three minutes to bleed to death from an arterial wound. Marcy had been living moments ago. Uncontrollable panic overwhelmed me. I dismissed calling the cops as quickly as it came to mind. After all, I wasn't the person my ID said I was, and I doubted my documents could hold up to any close inspection.

My prints were all over the house. There was no telling how many things I had touched during the course of my stay with her. The cops wouldn't believe I didn't kill her. Panic exploded in my brain. I did what every deer does who's ever been framed in the oncoming lights of a car. I froze. I blacked out on my feet. Poor Marcy! Sure, I was going to stay and loot the place for a couple of weeks. But no one deserved to die, and not ever like that.

When I came to, I walked out into the living room of the shabby apartment where I found my duffle on the living room couch, completely packed, with a bulging sealed envelope resting on top. I tore open the flap; inside was a bus ticket to Denver plus fifty-one hundred dollar bills. I called out into the empty apartment, "Who are you?"

The place was dead silent. The answer to my question was tucked in the envelope. I got dressed and walked out the door for the last time. Why did I take the ticket to Denver? I didn't have any other plans. Through most of the trip I slept and dreamed of the woman I called Red, and Marcy's eyes frozen with terror.

Thirty-nine weeks of the year Denver is one of the most beautiful cities on Earth. The snow-kissed mountains never look the same from day to day. The other thirteen weeks of the year a brown cloud hangs over the city like a pall. I arrived at the beginning of the wrong time of year.

When I walked out of the Denver bus station, a cab idled

by the curb. I opened the door. The driver must have been dozing because he damn near jumped out of his skin.

"Where's the best hotel around here?" I said as I got into the worn backseat.

"I'm to take you to the Brown Palace," he muttered sleepily.

"What did you just say?"

"The Brown Palace, sir! That's the best place around here."

I relaxed in the seat. "Cool. Take me there."

The mousy looking woman behind the check-in counter handed me the registration card. "Just sign at the bottom, sir. Everything else has been taken care of."

"Huh?"

"Just sign at the bottom, sir," she repeated. "Your stay has been paid for."

"By who?"

She squinted through her bifocals like I ought to know the answer to my question as well as anybody did. "I'm sorry Mr. Grimes, I really don't know, but if you like I can research it and call your room later."

Alone in my hotel room, I took my shoes off and lay down on the bed. The phone rang, and I assumed it was the front desk.

"Hello?" I said before the receiver made it to my ear.

"Well Paul, how do you find Denver so far?" came the throaty voice of a well manicured redhead I'd seen once before.

I tried to suppress my anger, "Polluted! What the hell is going on?"

"All in good time, Paul, why don't you shower, change, eat a wonderful meal and get a good night's sleep. I'll call you in the morning."

Then the line went dead.

That night I sat alone in my room with a bottle of Jack Daniels that I couldn't drink. I'd pour one and then stare at it until the ice melted, then throw it out and pour another.

The beeping ring of the phone woke me the next morning. "Hello, Paul! How are we feeling this morning?" Red sounded chipper.

Marcy came rushing back to me. "What the hell is going on? Why did you kill her that way? Who are you?"

She laughed. It reduced to a chuckle, she started talking. "I'll be by in an hour to pick you up, and we'll see about getting you some answers. You'll find some new clothes hanging in the closet. It's time you outgrew the T-shirts and jeans you're so fond of."

Once again, the line went dead.

I slammed the phone down and screamed in frustration. On the way to the bathroom I slid open the closet door and was shocked to see it packed with designer suits and shirts hanging above several pairs of high end shoes. How did the bitch know my sizes? The questions were piling up in my head.

I tried to make up my mind whether to stay in the room or go down to the lobby. If she came up to the room, I could beat the answers out of her and then decide what to do next. I stood by the door with my hand on the knob.

Before I could decide, the door burst open and she grabbed me by the wrist, locating a different pressure point with each of her four fingers and taking me to my knees on the carpet.

"You're about the dumbest Younger I've ever met," she laughed in my face.

"Please stop, please stop," I wheezed. She released me. "Who the hell are you?" I gasped.

"My name is Roberta Anderson," she said.

Ten minutes later we were out of the Brown Palace and sitting in the back seat of her limo.

"So, Bobby, would you mind telling me why all this is happening?"

"I can't tell you why. I can only tell you what I know."

Bobby looked to be in her early twenties. What the hell did she know about living? Bobby raised the partition separating us from the driver and started talking. "I know you have a lot of questions and I'll try to answer them all. But you have to listen because I'm only going to say all of this once.

"You want to know why you're a Younger. I don't have an answer for that one."

"You keep saying that," I moaned. "What the hell is a Younger?"

She waved off the question. "What I know is more Youngers are happening than ever before. You're the thirtieth one this century that I know of. For some reason our bodies stop, they just shut down, sometimes for hours, sometimes for days, and our genes do an about face. They go the other way. Doctors can't detect it, even if you find one who will believe you. Try it—you'll find out. I can't really tell you what you are, but let me tell you what you're not. You are not immortal. You can die of disease. A knife or bullet will put you in the ground."

She paused for a moment and then added, "You will start growing old again. It's like those old vinyl records. When the needle gets to a certain point in the groove, it bounces back to another one. Everybody's groove is different.

"You have to be careful when you restart though," she continued, "not that there's anything you can do. Anyone around will think you're dead. Twice I've woken up in the morgue, and the last time the mortician was six inches away from my abdomen with a scalpel. It takes longer and longer to relapse each time, hell, the first time happened overnight. With the population increasing, it's harder and harder to die alone, somewhere you'll be safe until you reset. The job's not getting any easier, kid."

I tried to absorb everything she said. Some of it made sense, most of it didn't. There were more questions I wanted to ask. "How do you know all this? How did you find out about me?"

Bobby's first answer made sense; her second disturbed the hell out of me, especially the way she smiled.

"My not so young friend, I'm a Younger myself. As far as knowing about you, there's a call that goes out when a Younger happens. It's a buzz inside your head. Kind of a warn—homing device." I let her stutter slide. I shouldn't have.

"How long have you been a Younger?"

Bobby leaned back into the car seat, closed her eyes and sighed as she said, "This is my eleventh trip, from age nineteen to age fifty-one. You do the math, I'm tired of it."

I leaned away and took a good look at her.

She blushed. "Any other questions?"

"You said there were thirty Youngers in this century. Where are they now?" Bobby turned to look out the window at the snow-covered foothills. She turned back to me, answering in a matter of fact tone. "They've passed on."

I panicked and tried the door handle. It moved but the door didn't. Childproof locks, my ass! They're victim-proof locks, in my opinion. She had her eyes closed. I heard her cluck gently.

"Relax! I didn't kill them—well not all of them."

For a moment, my imagination flashed to a Younger reunion. They could teach me the ins and outs of how to get rich and enjoy this wonderful gift. Now they were gone.

The car cut through the Colorado foothills. I remember passing wrought iron fencing standing twelve feet high with pillars of carved granite and signs that read, "Caution: Electrified Fencing."

The car rolled through the main gate. I caught a glimpse of her house through the century-old pine trees. She watched my face as she said, "Welcome to my humble abode." Like a twenty-two thousand square foot mansion could be called humble, or an abode.

The next three days were a crash course in my condition, a training camp for being a Younger. One evening, we were lying on lounge chairs by the indoor pool. Bobby had the sky light rolled back. Those sparkling stars, more points of light than I'd ever seen before, no longer looked so cold and far away. Together, Bobby and I could watch the passing of time. I was no longer bound to a beating clock. Passing seconds weren't the ticks of approaching pain and death anymore.

Bobby's voice broke through my thoughts. "Do you have any more questions?"

I'd been thinking about my next question for quite some time. "Why did you bring me here?"

There was a deep-tired sadness to her voice as she answered, "I want you to kill me!" This beautiful young woman, who had lived several centuries, wanted to die. I didn't know what to say. It was obvious by my silence.

"I suppose you want to know why?"

I didn't answer.

"I'm tired of living, Paul. After awhile, everything gets to be the same. There's nothing new in the world, except how small-minded people are. Rarely are they open to change. I've tried to change them. Have I told you why I killed the others?"

It was one of the many questions I asked during the last week and it was one she delayed answering.

"No, you haven't."

"They asked to be killed the same way I'm asking now. Remember me telling you a homing device goes off in your head whenever a Younger happens?"

I nodded.

"Up until the twentieth century there wasn't much you could do about it. Travel was limited. It took forever to get from one point to another, and by the time you got there either the Younger was insane, gone, or dead."

"How did they die?"

Bobby ignored me, and continued.

"Back then, it was actually harder to disappear. You grew up with your family and stayed within a few miles of your roots. Your neighbor was a hard five miles away, but you always had family. It's how we survived. The first time I grew young again I was almost burned at the stake for being a witch. That was during the time called the Enlightenment, back when the country was new and growing into its freedom. What a joke the whole mess was.

"A stranger freed me from my cell the night before my execution. Gordon was the first Younger I met. I fell in love with him instantly and fell out just as quickly when it came time to put him out of his misery. We were together almost seventy-five years."

Bobby made it sound like a marriage. One filled with love and understanding. I had no point of reference.

"The nineteenth century was a little better. The country was expanding by leaps and bounds. You could get to California, but it was a difficult and dangerous trip through country so hostile you slept with one eye open, even though you hadn't seen a soul in a month."

"Paul, are you listening to me?"

I answered honestly, "Not really."

I heard her mocking laughter and words mixed with mild disappointment. "You know, history does repeat itself over and over again. Someday you'll learn. Though I have a feeling it won't be for awhile. I'm tired. I'm going to bed." She rose from the lounge chair. Without a doubt, she was the most beautiful woman I've known. I was starting to hate the know-it-all bitch with a deep-rooted passion.

"Hey, Bobby."

"Yes?"

I had one more question for her. "How do you want to die?"

She looked down at me with those aqua eyes. For the first time I saw something in them I hadn't seen before. It was hope. She shrugged her shoulders. "It doesn't matter. It can be painful, messy or quiet, just so long as I'm dead."

The stars had been replaced by bright morning light when I got up off the lounge chair and headed off to bed. I walked into the guest bedroom, which was larger than the house I rented in Columbus, and found Bobby lying nude on top of the king size bed, asleep. Bright sunlight lit her unlined face. My gaze traveled up and down the length of her beautiful form. I felt an ache deep in my heart for this woman who had lived many lifetimes. It nibbled at the hate I felt for her. I leaned in close. "What are you doing here?"

Her eyes opened, and her arms gave me her answer as they wrapped themselves around my neck. She pulled me to her and whispered in my ear. "I don't want to sleep alone—do you mind?"

I pulled back quickly. "What are you, nuts? You asked me to kill you. Now you want to make love?"

I saw the shield drop behind those ancient eyes, revealing a loneliness so strong it went beyond description.

"Forgive me, I just needed the touch of my own kind," she said as she got off the bed and stalked out of the room. There was no chasing after her to tell her I was sorry. Exhaustion overtook me, so I stretched out on the bed and promptly fell asleep.

When I woke up, it was pitch black outside. The house was empty, not a stick of furniture anywhere, just the bed I was sleeping on and a small stool with a flashlight. I looked around for the light switch by the door. I hit the switch and nothing happened.

Something was terribly wrong. It wasn't just the fact that all signs of life had been removed from the house. I walked to the double front doors and saw a note taped to the dark oak wood.

Paul,
If you are reading this, then you know I'm gone.
You tripped an infrared beam when you stepped into the

foyer. You have approximately ten minutes before the
cops come and arrest you for trespassing. It takes them
that long to get up here from town. I suggest you get out
as fast as you can. There's a car parked outside the front
gate and if you leave right now you ought to make it with
a few minutes to spare.

The letter was signed *Good Luck*. I could hear her sarcastic
voice as I read the postscript at the bottom of the page:

You really are a stupid prick who has an awful lot
to learn. I don't think you'll live long enough to learn a
damn thing.

Jesse Owens would have had trouble keeping up with me as
I bolted out that door and ran down the half-mile driveway to a
gate that was closed and wrapped with a locked chain. On instinct,
my hands reached out to grab the iron bars so I could climb over
the top and drive away in the Mercedes 450SL parked on the
other side. My fingertips were a millimeter from the metal when I
remembered the signs on top of all the pillars. "Electrified Fence.
High Voltage."

"Bitch!" I screamed, disturbing an owl high up in one of
the pine trees that covered the landscape. The granite columns
supporting the gates could be climbed if you'd done that type of
thing before. The problem was I hadn't. My mind knew I would
probably fall, break a leg and spend the next few days in the county
hospital with a guard at my door.

Then it hit me. I was thinking like a sixty-year-old man and
not the early twenty-something Boss Stud Hoss I was. I jumped as
high as I could. Sweat broke out on my forehead as I strained to
reach the summit of stone. Two seconds later I was standing on top
of the column, looking out towards the city of Denver oppressed by

a layer of smog. In the distance, I could hear a car engine straining as it climbed the road to the house. I jumped, hit the ground, tucked and rolled to cushion the fall. My heart rapped against my chest.

I ran up to the car and was relieved when the door opened and keys rested in the ignition. I drove down the road thinking of all the different ways Roberta Anderson was going to die.

Blasting down the mountain road, taking the curves with the tires screaming for traction, a snippet from one of our conversations flashed in my brain. "You're not immortal. You can be killed . . ."

I backed off the gas and rode the brake pedal down that damn mountain.

When the clerk at the front desk told me the room charge hadn't been paid for the last three days, another of Bobby's morsels of wisdom came to mind. "Money is power! Once you have it, you can do almost anything. Without it, you're just another duck on the first day of hunting season."

I counted out twelve one hundred dollar bills, told the girl to keep the change and went up to my room to enjoy one last night in Denver's historic hotel. It took me a half a second to realize the door to my suite was slightly ajar as I slipped the electronic key into the metal slot. It was a half-second too long. I went flying through the air and crashed headfirst against the wall.

Bright purple lights flashed before my eyes, and I heard Bobby's sarcastic laugh. "Well, the cops didn't get you, so I guess it's my turn!"

I struggled to get to my feet.

"How the hell did you get in here?"

It was a stupid question to ask a woman who could move a mansion full of furniture in a day without waking me.

"You needed to be taught a lesson. Now let's get down to business before I lose all patience with you."

146

"And what business is that?"

"How are you going to kill me?"

At that moment a hundred different ways crossed my mind, most of them suitably painful and nasty.

"Why can't you kill yourself? Why do I have to do it?" I was pissed off and ready to kill the stupid bitch, but the proposition still didn't make sense.

For the second time since I'd met her, her eyes glistened with vulnerability, with humanity.

"I can't kill myself and neither can you. The same genetic switch that makes us younger also gives us a survival instinct far stronger than the average person. Whatever it is prevents us from destroying ourselves. Here, try it!"

She pulled a .380 short handgun from her pocket book and tossed it to me. "Go on, put it to your head and pull the trigger. I guarantee you won't be able to do it. Your body will stop you."

I looked down at the gun in my hand and back to the woman who had basically made my new life a living hell. "Ain't no way. You're not going to get me to kill myself and then walk away like there's nothing to it!"

Without thinking I tossed the gun back to her.

She caught it, pulled the slide back and put it to her temple in one smooth move. At first, nothing happened. Then I watched a slight tremor in her elbow start to build. A few seconds later, her whole body was shaking like a person with severe palsy. Sweat broke out on her forehead as the index finger of her right hand tried to put pressure on the trigger. Her skin turned pale white. Her eyes rolled back into her head. Slowly her knees began to buckle. A moment later I was bending over her fainted figure wondering if she was faking it or if the whole thing was true.

"Hey, are you all right?"

Her eyes fluttered open. The pupils dilated as they came back into focus. She whipped the gun around and placed it directly between my eyes. I backed off immediately.

"I am now." Her grimace told me she hadn't been faking it.

But I wasn't giving up so easily, I peppered her with scenarios. "Throw yourself in front of a car? Jump off a building? Take an overdose of . . . "

"Look, dumb shit! No matter what you or I try to do to ourselves, the survival instinct kicks in and stops us. I can't think of one way to fool it. And believe me when I say I've tried!"

Bobby did something at that moment I didn't think was possible for her. She cried, man how she cried. I would like to say that I held her and comforted her. But I didn't. She still had the gun in her hand and for the moment she wasn't the most stable of people. I guess my own survival instinct was taking charge. I stood there watching the loneliest woman in the world sob her heart out.

A little while later her sobs began to weaken. She sniffled like a little girl getting over a broken doll. "That's why you've got to kill me. I can't see it coming. Death has to be a surprise."

She followed me into the living room and plopped down on a genuine Victorian high-backed chair. My red headed sister in youth laid the gun down on the coffee table then let out a long sigh. For a flash, I could see the weight of her years in more than just her eyes as she began to talk.

"Paul, this is your first time being young, so for you it's new and exciting. But if you do it ten or twelve times, there's a deep dread when you approach the time to skip back again. Oh, there are things that keep it interesting for a while. Like all the new discoveries. When man landed on the moon, that was pretty amazing, but not as amazing as when Orville and Wilbur flew that box kite of a plane for the first time. In comparison to that, the moon landing was a logical progression. You've been around for a little while. Can you honestly say anything that's taken place in your lifetime came as any real surprise?"

I thought about it. I thought about it hard. I didn't want to tell her that for most of my life I'd been a very self-centered individual. If it didn't directly involve getting drunk or getting laid, I could have cared less about the world around me. Great triumphs in science didn't do a damn thing for me and great catastrophes did even less. All of them were outside my personal world.

"I guess not," I admitted.

Bobby looked up at me with the smirk I hated. "That's the difference between us. You guess not, and I know not! If you live long enough, you'll go through all kinds of stages. In this skip you'll probably try to nail every woman who walks. In the next skip you'll go after every man. Not because your sexual orientation changes, but because you'll be bored. You'll want to try something new and different. It will take a few skips to realize it's all the same. Wait until you fall in love with someone, I mean really fall in love with them, and know it's not going to last because they don't and you will. Do it four or five times, you won't bother anymore."

She looked down at the floor. I took her pause as a chance to ask a question.

"You said some of the others went insane. Why?"

She looked at me like a teacher looks at kid when he's been caught falling asleep in class. "Christ! How I hate to repeat myself. They went nuts because they couldn't face what happened. And what was going to happen." She paused. "Do you have any idea what the purpose behind a long life is?"

I shook my head "No."

"Well, that makes two of us!"

Bobby picked up an empty glass from the hotel end table, and hurled it at a painting. "When was the last time you dreamed about yourself as a child?"

I thought about it for a second before answering, "A week or so ago."

"Then more than likely the process has stopped. You're lucky, actually. I've seen a few skip back to childhood. They definitely went nuts. Imagine being a child with the mind of a man your age. You have all the knowledge of how life should be, but you're too young for anybody to listen to you."

"So why did you come here if you thought the police were going to get me?"

I watched her close her eyes and lean back into the chair. "People are the only game I have left, Paul. Most of mankind is so predictable it's frightening. But a few go off the charts and that's what makes it fun, for a while. You're just a game to me. A game I know is going to end, the way I want."

"If you know the outcome, then why are you screwing with me?"

Bobby looked at me and for the first time I could see a spark in those Dead Sea orbs. "There's a touch of unpredictability in you, not much, but a touch."

"So now that I've jumped through the first hoop, what's next?"

The spark blinked out in her eyes. Bobby dove for the gun resting on the table. She was fast. Damn fast!

"It's time for you to die!"

The survival instinct Bobby proved earlier kicked in like nitrous oxide. I jumped behind the sofa as two shots whizzed past my head. That 380 short sounded like a cannon going off inside the suite. The explosions from the gun punctuated her sick laughter.

I hugged the carpet, trying to figure a way out from behind the sofa without Bobby putting a slug in my back.

"You can get up, Paul. I'm not going to kill you. I just wanted to show you how good your survival instinct is."

I didn't relax my grip on that carpet. All she had to do was walk to the edge of the couch and pump a round into my trembling ass. "Screw you, bitch! I ain't moving."

I heard a click and the action slide back on the gun. A half-second later the clip hit me on top of my head.

"There! Does that make my little man feel better?"

It did. I flew over the back of the couch with arms extended, just like Superman. Soaring through the air, my flailing arms successfully hunted for her ivory neck. I screamed with joy as the soft flesh of her perfect neck condensed between my fingers.

That was seven lifetimes ago, seven lifetimes of a living hell. As Bobby's last breath wheezed out of her crushed larynx, the cops came crashing through the one-hundred-year-old door frame with their guns drawn. It took three of them to break my grip on Red's lifeless neck.

In a matter of weeks I was standing before a federal judge, sentenced to life in prison without parole for murdering Bobby. Within another week, they'd connected my fingerprints and DNA to Marcy in Savannah, and tacked a simultaneous life sentence on for good measure. I did not contest the charges, or even bargain. The gravity of such a sentence hadn't yet occurred to me.

When my lifetime relapsed once, the federal government grew interested in me. But by the third relapse, they lost interest. Every thirty-five years they still come by the federal prison to run their tests, they watch me die, and then wait for me to revive, but nobody cares.

I've exhausted every possible method of suicide, I've murdered other inmates and pleaded for the death penalty, but still I sit.

I sit, and I listen to Red laugh.

Acknowledgments

Columbus Creative Cooperative would like to thank all of the individuals and organizations that made this book possible. It was, without question, the product of many hands.

Thank you to the executive members of Columbus Creative Cooperative. Your insight into each other's work and spirit of collaboration is invaluable.

Thank you to all of the local businesses that have supported Columbus Creative Cooperative by retailing our books and sponsoring our work.

Thank you to our editors, Amy S. Dalrymple and Brad Pauquette, and a special thanks to Mallory Baker, for her superb proofreading.

Thank you to all of the authors who have ventured into our experiment in local literature.

Finally, thank you, dear reader, for appreciating and supporting local art. With the help of generous patrons like you, Columbus Creative Cooperative can continue to educate and encourage local writers, support local businesses and entertain the fantastic readers of Ohio.

For more information about Columbus Creative Cooperative, please visit **ColumbusCoop.org**.

About Columbus Creative Cooperative

Founded in 2010, Columbus Creative Cooperative is a group of writers and creative individuals who collaborate for self-improvement and collective publication.

Based in Columbus, Ohio, the group's mission is to promote the talent of local writers and artists, helping one another turn our efforts into mutually profitable enterprises.

The organization's first goal is to provide a network for honest peer feedback and collaboration for writers in the Central Ohio area. Writers of all skill levels and backgrounds are invited to attend the group's semi-monthly writers' workshops.

The organization's second goal is to print the best work produced in the region.

The co-op relies on the support and participation of readers, writers and local businesses in order to function.

Columbus Creative Cooperative is not a non-profit organization, but in many cases, it functions as one. As best as possible, the proceeds from the printed anthologies are distributed directly to the writers and artists who produce the content.

For more information about Columbus Creative Cooperative, please visit **ColumbusCoop.org**.

JEdward 💎 Warren
Jewelers

a little out of the way ...
... a lot out of the ordinary

Edward Warren Jewelers
1610 Cross Creeks Blvd
Pickerington, OH 43147
www.edwardwarrenjewelers.com
614-755-9229

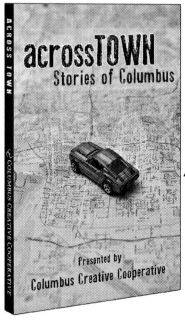